The Misfortune of Monsieur Fraque

I0540833

Paul Alexis

Translated By Richard Robinson

Sunny Lou Publishing Company
Portland, Oregon, USA
http://www.sunnyloupublishing.com

1st Edition, 24 November 2021

ISBN: 978-1-955392-19-8

# # #

This translation from French is based on the G. Charpentier, Éditeur, 2nd edition of *La fin de Lucie Pellegrin, L'infortune de Monsieur Fraque, Les femmes du père Lefèvre, Journal de Monsieur Mure,* Paris, 1880.

Contents

Dedication by the Translator

To my mother, Patricia (Patsy) née Butchart, who passed this year, and who would have loved to read this story about Monsieur Fraque and "old" France, if for nothing else than for the nostalgia of it – if I had only gotten it published and in her hands sooner; and to her mother, my grandmother, Helen, née Sweetland, who passed nearly twenty-five years ago, and who preferred detective stories to Naturalism, but would have read this story anyways, if for no other reason than that I had asked her to. Because that's how it works when you love someone. May they both rest in the peace they deserve and have long deserved, without desecration, beside the God or the thing they believed in. And may the United States of America, one nation under God, not so indivisible anymore, and Canada (where they hailed from), and Western Europe where we all ultimately trace our roots to – may they all fare well in the near future and continue to exist in some recognizable form for the decades, and who knows, for the centuries to come, with the customs and the manners we loved, and love, in spite of their imperfections and in spite of all the hatred and ingratitude sprouting up these days from every quarter, in all places, like weeds casting shade.

– Richard Robinson, 23 November 2021

Introduction

I knew Monsieur Fraque as well. That octogenarian sitting up straight in the saddle, stands out against the backdrop of my childhood memories. His eccentricity bordering on madness, his manias, his raising of pigs, his bizarre phrases, none of this is invented. With these facts furnished by reality, what did I do? I imagined a long "conjugal misfortune" was the cause of this breakdown, and I have endeavored to reconstitute the phases of that misfortune. But my hand was, then, quite inexperienced for such a task. The depiction of Madame Fraque has remained in outline during her youth and her older years. Instead of going into the complete truth of these individuals, I have contented myself with indicating some of their aspects, seen often from a comical angle. Such as it is, this study is merely a sketch of a novel on the provinces, achieved with great effort three years ago (1876), by a young man who was expecting to have, and had, a difficult job of it.

– Paul Alexis

Chapter 1

The Fraques descended from a hamlet off the beaten path, in the mountains, from a country of wolves, whose inhabitants, going back to some common author, are today still "the Fraques." The great-grandfather, an illiterate peasant like all his more-or-less distant cousins, sent his son from time to time "to learn" from the curate at the canton's county seat, forty kilometers away. This boy, at the time of his father's death, around 1750, one fine morning, with fifty *ecus* tied up in his handkerchief, disembarked at Noirfond, capital of a province in France's *midi*, seat of a parliament and of a bishopric. At first, metropolitan canter, then clerk to a public prosecutor, he wedded a bailiff's daughter, and finished by becoming a clerk of the parliamentary court. Ultimately, his son, the father of M. Fraque, having been raised among official documents, but dispossessed of his paternal charge by the Revolution, was a man of great merit, a provincial Talleyrand, a purchaser of national property, by and by professor of law, imperial prosecutor and counsellor under the First Empire. During the Hundred Days he was on the verge of being made a prefect. But from the Second Restoration, having become definitively monarchist, he became a member of Parliament, and then first president of the Royal Court of Noirfond. Had he belonged to the nobility, those days then, a similar man would have doubtless risen higher. When death stopped him in his ascension, he was on the verge of becoming noble, which had been made easier twenty-five years earlier by the stroke of genius of his marriage. At the height of the Terror, the Jacobin Fraque, foreseeing that in France the vanquished of today would sooner or later become the vanquishers of tomorrow and that it is good to have a foot in both camps, made the seeming folly of marrying the *ci-devant*[1] Hélène de Beaumont, orphan and last descendent of that illustrious family, while at the same time purchasing the antique and superb Hôtel de Beaumont for a song.

The sole offspring of this crossbreeding, the young Hector, had grown up in the aristocratic mansion doing as he pleased. He lost his mother early in life. Only at meal hours did he see his father, sallow in complexion, speaking little, absorbed. Except on five or six important days out of the year, when the first president gave a dinner for the magistrates in his jurisdiction, the furniture of the immense halls remained hidden under covers of grey lustring. The thick damask curtains blocked the daylight from entering the rooms. And, under the great chestnut trees in the garden, grass invaded the walkways between the neglected flowerbeds; the bowers had turned into impenetrable thickets; moss and dead leaves clogged the large pond; and the statues themselves, standing here and there, dirty and dark like neglected statues, seemed to yawn with boredom. Knowing few children his own age, always alone among the domestics, Hector, in this not very recreative environment, had become gloomy and brusk, uncompromising, teasing, quarrelsome, loving nothing but horses and weaponry, bickering even with the dogs. At secondary

---

[1]*ci-devant*: literally "former", but has particular reference to aristocrats who lost their title during the French Revolution.

school, where his father had sent him belatedly, the young Fraque had a acquired a reputation for being wrongheaded: insolent with his professors, arguing with his teachers, grappling with his peers. Small in stature, more furious than strong, he was usually beaten in fact, and returned home with several lumps on his face, nail scratches on his cheek. The scuffles made his delicate, little hands bleed. Deep down, underneath the combative attitudes, Hector was the best boy in the world. M. Fraque, his father, who had divined the sheep in wolf's clothing, had the greatest contempt for his son, in whom he saw every bit of his late wife reviving.

The young Fraque earned his bachelor's degree, and began his study of law at the Faculty of Noirfond; when the first president, his father, died, he was already in his tenth term. At twenty-two years old, alone and free in life, master of a pretty fortune, M. Fraque consecrated a suitable amount of time to mourning his father and to a genuine affliction, then left for Paris like a fool. He spent six years there before passing his fourth examination and presenting his thesis; at the end of six years, always keeping himself healthy and strong like a young oak, it was discovered that this prodigal, but reasonable, son had only spent his annual rents, in addition to incurring twenty thousand francs of debt. The liquidation of his follies of youth diminished consequently very little of his capital. Then, before his thirtieth year, having grown wise, M. Fraque thought only about returning to Noirfond.

He had had enough of Paris. Paris, where he

had nothing to do, weighed on him; M. Fraque was born "provincial." Lost in that busy and indifferent crowd of people, where nobody paid attention to him, having neither a passion nor a great ambition to keep himself occupied, being isolated, he got bored. It is not that M. Fraque remained indifferent to the events of his times, or to the thrust of his generation. He read the journals. He was liberal like all youth were during the reign of Charles X, within the limits of the charter. He frequented M. Thiers and M. Mignet, his fellow students, whom he had known in Provence, at the college and faculty of law. He paid a visit from time to time to M. Guizot. But fine enough in his sensibilities to sense by imperceptible nuances that these ambitious, active and lively young men, didn't take him seriously, and wounded by a thousand small pin pricks over the course of the long period of friendships, M. Fraque acknowledged to himself that, being too proud to resign himself in so vast a theatre to secondary roles, it would be better for him to return to the countryside where he would easily play the first.

And, one fine morning in September 1829, all the windows of the Hôtel de Beaumont were thrown open to let the sun joyously enter, to evaporate the odor of mold and stuffiness. Towards noon, the old concierge, standing for a long time on the sill, suddenly removed his cap. His young master was not more than thirty paces from the paternal home. Hector went straight up to the room where his father and mother had died, the room that would now become his own, looked for a moment at the two oil portraits whose tones had been altered by humidity, washed his face and hands, and shook off the dust of the journey. Several minutes later, in the garden, the dead leaves of the large chestnut trees crunched loudly under the feet of the traveller. He had himself driven to a restaurant for dinner. The following day, he didn't go outside, was nostalgic for Paris a little, hired a valet and a chef. Two days later, on Sunday, at the afternoon mass in Saint-Jean Church, all members of Noirfond's high society turned their heads: M. Fraque, freshly shaven and completely dashing, was standing near the door, before the font. At the exit, each person, while passing by, greeted him. Two old counselors who, at the first president's dinners, had seen M. Fraque as a little child, shook his hand.

"Here you are, returned at last!..." they said, nodding their head.

Young men his same age, with a disquieted curiosity, added:

"Is it for good?"

Chapter 2

In the little town, the news of his return spread like wildfire.

One hour after mass, M. Fraque was finishing his lunch. Suddenly a tall old man, with a white beard, a stranger, rushed into the dining room, pushing aside the valet, and flew into the arms of the young man, while exclaiming:

"Hector, my dear, embrace your uncle!"

Stupefied, M. Fraque received at first a big caress on either cheek, like a child. It took him a moment of reflection before he recognized M. Marquis de Grandval, a distant relative of his mother. He had not seen him but four times at most in his life. The old gentleman, while M. Fraque père was alive, had never treated him in this fashion as a nephew, the son of "that Jacobin, that purchaser of national property, that upstart, whom the last of the de Beaumont hadn't the shame of associating with." But Hector didn't have time to get upset by these recollections. M. de Grandval didn't let him open his mouth. Kissed, pampered, adulated, dazed, subjugated by the whirlwind of an old man, Hector ended up by picking up his hat and his gloves, and going out with his new uncle. Ten minutes later, M. de Grandval introduced the young man into his bankrupt marquis' home. In a corner of the sitting room, Zoé had taken up again, for the occasion, an aquarelle that had been set aside when she left the convent four years earlier.

Several days later, M. Hector Fraque was seen passing along the Promenade, giving his arm for the first time in public to his "cousin" Zoé de Grandval. They were commented on at first in front of multiple cafes, where regulars observed them, seated at outside tables, not consuming anything. Doctor Boisvert, a member of the circle, peddled the news all hot off the press at various homes in the suburb of Saint-Germain and de la Chaussée-d'Antin of Noirfond. One also heard about it soon enough in the reading room. The afternoon was not over when some people were already smiling about it in the Pas-Perdus Hall of the Palace of Justice. Finally, by evening, all the town was talking about the marriage of "Fraque the son, back in town, you know him..." with Mademoiselle de Grandval, "his cousin if you will..."

Small-town gossips invent stories in the beginning; then, what they have invented ends up becoming true. M. Fraque, who was not a sot, saw through, like anyone else, this marquis' game of coming to shove his only daughter in his face like that. He made a promise to himself to never bite at the conjugal bait. But the provinces offer so few distractions! How was he going to spend the long evenings of his first winter faraway from "the capital," and why not profit from the infinite distractions of an intimate comedy that involved a constant battle of the wits. He made his decision immediately. He refused none of M. de Grandval's advances, dined at his house every Sunday, passed entire evenings together, returned his polite gestures in game[2], in small gifts to Mademoi-

---

[2]in game: *en gibier* – presumably he returned the marquis' favors by gifts of game (venison, fowl, etc.) he had captured while

selle Zoé which could have passed for engagement gifts. He felt a veritable charm, an unusual tickling of his self-esteem, to see himself the object of the considerations and secret desires of these two beings. Zoé was certainly far from pretty. Beneath the thinness of her body of a pensioner, one divined a dry and positive soul, gifted with a fierce will, a sour-tempered firmness. But she was a young woman, after all. In terms of race, intelligence, education, she was superior to all the women he had frequented thus far in his life as a bachelor. Finally, what piqued his pleasure most was this Machiavellian thought: "I'll fool them, this hard-up marquis ruined by gambling and his ugly daughter." He even went so far as to say, one evening, after returning to Hôtel de Beaumont: "I have half a mind to write to my friends in Paris, that while they are there, preparing for the ascension to power of the bourgeoisie, I am here, in the act of conning the nobility."

M. Fraque had a strong opponent. Two months passed. Christmas was approaching. The marquis came, one morning, to invite Hector over to his house for Christmas Eve dinner. M. Fraque arrived at six thirty in the evening, rather sullen. He had had himself registered with the Noirfond bar during the day. The dead calm and inertia of these first weeks of life in the provinces were weighing down on him. He had already grown tired of the comedy the marquis was putting on for him. Before they sat down at the table, Mademoiselle de Grandval showed him the aquarelle begun at the convent, completely finished.

---

hunting?

Hector showed so little admiration for it that he was impolite. Zoé went to look for her album, didn't spare him any drawing, even gave him a sepia, which M. Fraque shoved brusquely into his pocket. Zoé didn't seem to notice; she was all happy and all smiles while taking Hector's arm to go into the dining room.

M. Fraque looked at her several times out of the corner of his eye. He was surprised: Zoé was no longer ugly. Her large nose no longer shocked him. Her hair looked nice. Her dark eyes emitted a surprising luster: they were all he saw! Her black satin dress, with an old-fashioned shape, strange, worn carelessly, had character. An enormous Noel log burned in the fireplace, tainted the ceiling rosy. The table was served, with some remnants of old luxury. The marquis had found in his once-celebrated wine cave some last bottles, which M. Fraque did the honor of opening. After coffee, around ten o'clock, Hector was not upset when the marquis left them to spend an hour at the circle, while waiting for the midnight mass which Zoé wished to attend. But he could hardly profit from this first face to face.

Zoé had his cigar lit.

"Now, I didn't tell you, cousin, I cannot chat with you this evening, I... am on retreat. But I will play some music for you. Make yourself comfortable in this armchair."

And she began to play the piano, one of those antique square pianos, from the days of the Empire. It was missing some chords. Certain notes made a cracked, clavecin-like sound. She only played old

Christmas carols. When the marquis returned from his circle, they left for Saint-Jean.

The church was full. The organ played the same tunes that Mademoiselle de Grandval had plonked out on the old piano. They sat down, all three of them, the marquis between the two young people, on the Grandval family's worm-eaten bench. The marquis was radiant: he must have won several louis at the circle. Zoé subsequently knelt down and remained the whole time that they were there in prayer, her face in her hands. Hector thought about his midnight mass the year before, in Paris. With some young men and women, he had entered La Madeleine. The were unable to proceed ten steps because of the crowd and departed to get supper. When Mademoiselle de Grandval rose to take communion, M. Fraque followed her with his eyes. She walked with her head lowered, hands joined, very contemplative. Then, for the first time, this thought was formulated in M. Fraque's mind:

"Why, in fact, would I not marry her?"

The next day, on awakening, the idea seemed completely ludicrous to him. And he didn't think about it again.

Chapter 3

He looked for other distractions. He even took a small trip to Marseille, where he passed five days with an old classmate, – who was the lover of the Grand-Théatre's Dugazon.[3] On his return, he remained another three weeks without setting foot in the Marquis de Grandval's house. But the marquis, to his great astonishment, didn't come looking for him. To Hector, his absence was worse than several months of intimacy.

At first, he grew bored. In the evening, he felt he was missing something. It didn't matter how many walks along the Promenade he made, smoking cigars. He didn't visit the cafes. He had himself received at a circle, not the one that the marquis went to; but, not liking the game, Hector was compelled to return home at a decent hour. And, as he was in the habit of going to bed late, when the three or four journals he subscribed to had been thoroughly glanced through since morning, he had nothing else to do but stoke the fire. While he was fiddling with the fire tongs, his thoughts returned to the marquis' family: – "She really wasn't bad at the midnight mass, kneeling... She prays with the devout ardor of a Spaniard... The two of them ought to be feeling quite conned no longer to see me! When then should I go to enjoy the disappointment on their faces?..."

One Sunday, he couldn't resist. One hour be-

---

[3]Dugazon: in comic operas, the actress playing the roles of lover and maid.

fore dinner, he rang at the Grandval's door. His heart was beating a little. How to explain his long absence? He didn't have to explain anything at all. Zoé received him with the most natural attitude. The marquis was beaming, with that feverish joy that is common among gamblers: he had played dealer all afternoon with an incredible vein of luck. From time to time, at the table, he buried his pinky into this fob to touch the three five-hundred-franc bills that he had won. After desert, he didn't even enter the salon, kissed Zoé on the forehead, extended his hand to his nephew, and returned to his circle.

M. Fraque took his coffee in the salon, in a tête-à-tête with Zoé. He couldn't find anything of much importance to tell her. To hide his embarrassment, he went to light the candles on the piano.

"Cousin," he implored her in the most pleasant of tone of voice, "if you should play for me a second time those pretty Christmas carols..."

"Cousin," she responded seriously, "this evening I'm not on retreat anymore. I will tell you what I would have told you the other day, three weeks ago, if I had been able to."

M. Fraque was completely taken aback.

"Where does she plan to go with this?" he wondered to himself anxiously.

In her dry tone of voice, with much self-assurance, she made it known to him that she was putting an end to their recent intimacy. They were in a small town. Everyone knew each other. And rumors that didn't please her were beginning to fly. M. Fraque, discountenanced, felt like he was listening to a young widow.

She apologized even that it was not her father who was having this talk with M. Fraque. But hadn't she become accustomed, early in life, to take care of herself! This very evening, she would communicate her resolution to the marquis, who would have no choice but to accept.

"I don't understand you," stammered the young man from time to time. "What sort of rumors?..."

Zoé explained herself even more boldly. She spoke to him of his fortune. She made him understand that a poor de Grandval did not marry a rich Fraque. She added even that she was going to become a nun:

"Without rancor, cousin, let's part as good friends."

And she held out her hand to him. Then she smiled:

"I would like you to attend my taking-the-veil ceremony."

Become serious again, she made a low farewell curtsey:

"I will pray for your happiness all my life."

And she retired to her room. Hector, stupefied, annoyed, and taken however by a crazy impulse to laugh, didn't leave immediately. His first thought was

to wait for the marquis' return, to tell him everything
he didn't have the presence of mind to say to Zoé.
The lamp was smoking, he turned it down. He blew
on the fire for a while. Then he went to the piano to
play *Malborough s'en va-t'en guerre* with one finger.
In the end, he lost patience and departed, closing the
doors violently behind him.

Zoé, without fire in her room, came back
quickly, and installed herself in the armchair that M.
Fraque had just quit. She put a last log in the fireplace, she warmed her hands for a long time, – while
watching the bright flames. And she finished by falling asleep. The marquis returned around two in the
morning, in a bad mood, slamming the doors himself,
completely cleaned out. Zoé, her eyes wide open
again, recounted slowly to her father the manner in
which she had believed it her duty to dismiss Hector.

The marquis, overwhelmed, let himself fall
into an armchair. Instead of responding, he passed his
hand over his face. He was sweating. Then he flew
into a rage against their poverty. Their silver was at
the Mont-de-Piété[4] since the beginning of the month.
He was going to be two years behind payment on in-
terest with his big creditors. It was well known, and
the manager of the circle had just refused him one
hundred francs this afternoon. Now, after that affront,
here's his daughter who, without consulting him, has
compromised perhaps their last resource.

At that moment, she came and took both his
hands, and said to him:

---

[4]Mont-de-Piété: one of a chain of pawn shops.

"Don't be angry, father. You'll see... Everything will sort itself out."

Suddenly, the old gambler rose, transported:

"You are an angel, you!" he exclaimed while holding his daughter in his arms.

Zoé had just slid into his fob something heavy, some gold: her savings as a young girl rolled up in paper.

At the same hour, M. Fraque was still pacing far and wide in his vast room. The candle, on the nightstand, no longer emitted, in the middle of the darkness, but the feeble light of a glowworm. M. Fraque didn't know what to do. He was angry with that ugly convent escapee for having troubled him like this. He felt something of a rage to see her once again "to tell her what's what." At moments, he felt something of a doubt vacillating inside him as to the girl's sincerity. And the poor fellow even came to the point of wishing that Zoé had lied when she said she couldn't accept him. Towards morning, this fever abated. He blew out the candle and lay down on the bed with his clothes on. Facing the alcove where his bed was located, the picture frames of his father and mother's portraits stood out in the pallor of a new day. M. Fraque made up his mind finally. Then, having calmed down, he daydreamed that the first president Fraque was smiling and approved of his son, he who had married, the first in their family, a noble girl without a fortune.

That same day, with a triumphant smile, Zoé

held out to the marquis a letter whose seal she recognized. Several instants later, Hector, dressed to the nines, with grey gloves on, came in person to speak with the Marquis de Grandval. There was nothing bourgeoise about it, he offered two hundred thousand francs in dowry for Mademoiselle de Grandval's hand in marriage. Zoé's insinuation, – " a poor de Grandval did not marry a rich Fraque" – produced its effect.

The marquis was completely beside himself with joy when he ran to announce the great news to his daughter. It seemed to him that he had just recovered in one minute all the gambling losses of his lifetime.

Zoé remained cold, disdainful.

Chapter 4

The preparations were rushed. The great day arrived, one rainy, chilly day in March. There was a big wind. The marriage at the town hall took place towards midnight. At twelve thirty, carriages showed up before Saint-Jean. The church was full. In spite of the wind, in spite of the advanced hour, all of Noirfond was there: nobility, bourgeoisie, commoners. A thousand curious glances were directed at Mademoiselle de Grandval. There was a single voice of opinion: she was found to be inelegant and ugly behind the wedding veil. During mass, the church was full of comings and goings and whispers. Zoé, who sensed all this disapprobation behind her back, looked pale in her lace. The naïve satisfaction painted on Hector's face annoyed her.

She was angry with him for being foolishly infatuated with her. She was angry with him for not being noble. She pushed the injustice to the point even of being angry with him for having made her wealthy. Towards the conclusion, according to custom, M. Fraque escorted her into the lateral chapel, before the altar of the Holy Virgin. Zoé, kneeling, while performing her act of consecration, looked at him again. He wasn't ugly in his new outfit. His ashen blond hair, which hung down long and straight, gave him a gentle physiognomy. It was at that moment that she felt completely disposed to making life difficult for him.

In the sacristy, the marquis embraced the new-

lyweds, gave them his benediction. And they departed
for Hôtel de Beaumont, alone. In the carriage, M.
Fraque leaned over to give his wife her first marriage
kiss. Zoé moved away. Nobody ever knew what happened exactly on their wedding night. M. Fraque never spoke about it. Only, later, M. Fraque became hard
of hearing, and malignant persons of Noirfond always
claimed that his deafness originally dated from a total
excess of emotions on that inauspicious night.

As long as her father was alive, Madame
Fraque didn't give too much cause for gossip however. Unfortunately for M. Fraque's conjugal tranquili-
ty, one night, the old gambler was brought home from
his circle after having been seized by an attack as the
result of a failed martingale[5]. With the marquis dead,
Zoé no longer restrained herself. She didn't slide into
adultery; she penetrated it resolutely, just as she had
entered into marriage, cold and calculating. In her
case there was neither impulse nor fall. If she was often enticed by her senses, hatred for her husband was
a still more powerful motive. If M. Fraque had found
her virtue disagreeable, Zoé would have been able to
remain virtuous.

The first time, M. Fraque took the thing badly.
Naturally, he didn't discover the truth until later: all
Noirfond was already pointing their finger at him.
The scandal was all the greater after M. Fraque had
been nominated suddenly attorney general of Noirfond, because of the influence of his Parisian friends
who had become all powerful following the July revolution. The new magistrate's anger was tragic. There

---

[5]martingale: a gambling technique of doubling down after a loss.

was a duel, in Nice, which was not yet annexed. The lover came away without so much as a scratch: the husband returned home with his arm in a sling. The sword had pierced it through and through.

The laughers laughed all more loudly. It wasn't, moreover, until much later that people began to feel sorry for M. Fraque, precisely at that moment when he had finally resigned himself to carry his conjugal cross with dignity. He never asked for a physical separation. Doubtless, there was some secret drama there, one of those unavowed, inexplicable sentiments. He preferred to play indifferent. There you have it, the singular "unfortunate husband" whom he was quickly to become.

Well in advance of forty years old, M. Fraque lacked discernible age, he had put so much effort into looking older. He would have died his hair white if nature had not been so kind as to make his pale blond locks turn silver early. Soon promoted to Crown prosecutor, he was condemned in perpetuity to wearing the white tie and, as was the custom then, the blue outfit with the large cuffs with metal buttons. Morally, he wore the white tie also: M. Prudhomme, in the Palace of Justice, busting sage lances in an effort to defend propriety, religion and family, while at the same time, in his private life, that methodical white tie was crumpled by a maniacal originality, and a shrill eccentricity.

Monsieur passed his life in one wing of the Hôtel de Beaumont, and Madame in the other. The great, immense reception hall, with its panels painted by Boucher, and a veritable stage at the back, on

which M. Fraque's maternal great-grandmother had
played everything Marivaux[6] had written, the dining
room and the long gallery of tableaux, – all in all fifteen windows of facade, – separated the two spouses.
Each morning, toward nine o'clock, Isnard, the *valet
de chambre*, entered the room of his master who, in-
variably, this latter, often even before having opened
his eyes, addressed to his valet the same two ques-
tions: – "How's my mare doing? Do you know if
Madame slept well?" And almost immediately, feign-
ing not to hear the response, exaggerating his deafness, M. Fraque vociferated: "Good beast! Good
beast!" And he didn't stop talking about his mare, all
the while Isnard spent dressing him: "The night was
cold, she didn't catch a cold? Her woolen cover, is it
sufficient for her?" Isnard had forgotten one day to
give her her oats and a piece of sugar and that was all
it took for Isnard to be chased out of the room! It was
simply that he loved his animals "more" than people,
and he would rather lose a "relative than a mare...."
At eleven o'clock, the bell sounded for breakfast, and
M. Fraque passed into the dining room. Evening and
morning, the place for Madame was set. But, each
year, she didn't eat but thirty times face to face with
her husband.

Soon this human affection for his mare no
longer sufficed for M. Fraque. He had a greyhound.
He placed in his study a large cage, where canaries
nested. Over the years, this passion for animals grew
to such proportions that after having been called to
preside over an agricultural show in a small neighbor-

---

[6]Marivaux: Pierre de Marivaux, 18th century French playwright.

ing town, M. Fraque returned with the whim for raising pigs.

Chapter 5

Madame Fraque had just then turned thirty. Far from having grown calm with age, this willful woman and her excesses, into which figured such a large hatred of her husband, had only exasperated things. Whereas formerly, when M. Fraque had returned from Nice with a sword wound, that bravery had appeared ridiculous to her, that jealousy odious, – today she reproached the same man with being feeble, complacent, cowardly. She had never been beautiful. Her hair grew thinner. She had bad teeth. She had never seemed so thin. She was surprised and angered to believe that her victim escaped her. Her husband's existence was no longer without purpose.

At four kilometers from Noirfond, just off the road to Marseille, M. Fraque possessed a beautiful piece of land which he had visited two times a year if that. One Saturday evening, he received word from the farmer: – the twelve male and female pigs that the Crown prosecutor had purchased at the agricultural show had arrived. And the farmer, extremely embarrassed, had lodged them provisionally in the stable and in the shed, where the twelve couples soiled everything, making a dreadful racket.

On the following day, in the early hours of the morning, Isnard woke his master up, who mounted a horse, and proceeded at a trot to his property. M. Fraque took fifteen days of absence from work, which he spent with his pigs, touching them, caressing them, giving them their acorns, like a child taking great pleasure in hearing them snort, fart, and sniff. Their bellies, from which hung long smooth bristles, were deformed. They plunged their snout with delight into their swill of bran and potatoes. M. Fraque laughed himself to tears, and had completely forgotten his wife.

An architect, sent from Marseille, arrived at the moment when the Crown prosecutor, beaming, was in the process of whispering sweet nothings into the ear of a young sow. In the middle of discussions, while they were looking for a site, he halted plans to build a model pigsty. Instead of a pigsty, M. Fraque wanted a palace. Nothing would be more beautiful! It had to have marble everywhere and nothing but marble, pink marble for the troughs, white marble for the interior stairs, green marble for the columns of the facade and the emblematic sculptures of the pediment. When M. Fraque had returned from his land, at the end of fifteen days, his happy and beaming attitude stupefied Zoé.

And, for six months, he went everyday to his "*Villa-Poorcels*" to oversee masons and architect, sculptors and marble masons. He was often missing at court hearings. As soon as he exited the public prosecutor's office, he jumped into the saddle. He got fat. On the day of inauguration of the pigsty, there was at "*Villa-Poorcels*" a great agricultural celebration which, naturally, Madame Fraque refused to attend. The prefect, the first president, the bishop himself, Doctor Boisvert, several members of the regional counsel, took breakfast at the pigsty. Suddenly, at dessert, when the champagne bottles were uncorked, the doors were opened and the inhabitants of the new palace, covered in ribbons and pink garlands, erupted onto the scene snorting with joy. There was a toast, speeches, a brass band, an open air dance, and finally, in the evening, fireworks. The great fireworks cannon displayed, for all to see, in the sky, the image of a gigantic pig.

This solicitude for the porcine race progressed with M. Fraque to a state of mild chronic madness. It cost him a lot of money, almost as much as his wife's toilette. His forty thousand livres of rent were no longer enough. He was even forced to make a dent from time to time in his capital, so that his cherished pigs might live like princes. But he was completely absorbed in them. His pigs replaced his necessities of distraction, his needs for women. In their company, he forgot his friends back in Paris, who had become all powerful, academicians, ministers. By raising them, his pigs, this philosopher husband desensitized for years his conjugal wound. Old age arrived. He became very patient, very content, very learned. He exaggerated arbitrarily his deafness from birth, which acted like a wall that he erected between the rest of the world and his willful egoism. Planning not to see anything, he judged it prudent not to hear anything. He pushed to excess the Anglomania that made him call his country estate "*Villa-Poorcels*" and his new mare "Miss Jenny." He embellished now his least of phrases with English expressions. He no longer ate anything but English cuisine. His dream was to pass for a "perfect gentleman," an eccentric, full of haughtiness, an improver of swine and a misanthrope.

Chapter 6

Zoé, whom the new attitude of her husband disquieted, and who had just rounded the critical cape of forty
years, had for some time now bestowed her friendship
on one of the substitute Crown prosecutors. That was
already of public notoriety. And Noirfond's open
minds had a field day with the word "substitute."
Much more spiritual, Mr. Fraque "saw" nothing, contented himself with supporting his substitute's appli-
cation for the cross, and recommended him to the
ministry. The substitute obtained the Legion of Honor
and was nominated for a position at Lyon. That
turned the table, and the laughers switched sides,
laughing at Zoé. Looking away, taciturn, with pursed
lips, Zoé bided her time.

Several weeks before his marriage, M. Fraque
had been the godfather of his farmer's son. It didn't
take long before the little Firmin was a handsome
young man, tall, tan and trim. His father brought him
along to Hôtel de Beaumont each time he came to cart
wood, wine or oil. M. Fraque pinched his godson's
cheek and gave him a coin worth forty sous. Later, he
had obtained for him a grant at the école des Frères.[7]
Firmin spent four years there, and left with superb
handwriting and a no-contest grand prize for calligra-
phy. The Crown prosecutor, having need sometimes
of a beautiful handwriting to make copies of certain
documents, became attached to the small farmer as
his secretary. Firmin wasn't yet seventeen years old.

---

[7]école des Frères: a school for boys coming from families without
the means to pay for it.

He was a child, very slender, with a slightly dark skin, but a quick and ardent eye. A nascent down softened with blue the roundness of his lips. M. Fraque wasn't too happy with him. Firmin, who was very lazy, spent his time in a small room in front of his master's office using his quill to cover blank sheets of paper with large arabesques. In order to surprise him in the act, M. Fraque sometimes entered on tippy toe and pulled on his ears.

One afternoon, returning from the palace, the Crown prosecutor was less surprised than irritated to find his little clerk missing from his work table. The door to his office was only pushed closed. He opened it brusquely with the end of his cane. And he suddenly grew red in the face. Madame Fraque in a loose fitting dressing gown was still extended on the leather couch where M. Fraque, on summer afternoons, took a siesta. Firmin, completely ashamed, got up and fell on his knees against the wall, hiding his face in his hands.

M. Fraque didn't hesitate but for one second. He was forced to "see," this time, and he couldn't decorate the child. He went and seized Firmin by the ear and contented himself by throwing him out the door, saying to him:

"So young, Monsieur, and without being forced to..."

When Mr. Fraque returned, his wife was upright. She looked him straight in the face, and withdrew.

However cruel and strong she demonstrated herself to be, she took to bed for three days, and to her room for six weeks. One night of insomnia, for the first time in many years, she wept. The following day, after having, as was her habit, gobbled up her two raw eggs and chocolate in bed, she had her mirror brought to her. Her eyes were large and protruding. She noticed how dreadful she looked. Her bones, now, were poking out through the skin.

It was quite finished. She could no longer wear, in the evenings, merely a low-cut dress.

Chapter 7

For fifteen or eighteen months, M. Fraque breathed.

Madame Fraque in several weeks had aged ten years. Madame Fraque no longer dyed her hair, no longer put on makeup, had renounced the flashy toilette and bright dresses. Madame Fraque no longer accepted invitations, no longer made visits, barred her door, only receiving two or three old women, both noble and devout. Filled at first with a secret joy, later exuberant, visibly younger by the sudden aging of his wife, M. Fraque soon became less deaf, walked more erect, forgot to speak with English jargon, neglected his pigs and his mare. This was the most active and most brilliant period in his life. The misanthrope of yesterday became interested in man now. The revolution of February had just dethroned Louis-Philippe. Even though all his youthful sympathies were attached to the fallen regime, M. Fraque, "ceding to the solicitations of conservatives, and wanting to ensure order," had, as Crown prosecutor, become chief prosecutor. And he had been elected lieutenant-colonel of the National Guard. In the peaceable town of Noirfond, order was nowise called into question. But this grownup child, who had stopped feeling miserable, had the opportunity to play soldier: ever on horseback and in uniform, giving orders in a curt tone of voice, conducting reviews with the greatest seriousness, commanding marches and military reconnaissances. People made fun of him at first, asking where the eternal, white cravat and inevitable outfit with its metal buttons had gotten off to. They ended up by taking him seriously; the women thought he had a "military air;" the people believed in his liberalism.

While the triumphant M. Fraque in this way acquired popularity, a second youth, – Madame Fraque made herself forgotten. Of her many worldly habits, she had conserved only that of promenades by carriage. She always loved to feel herself rolling along for one or two hours, on some main road on beautiful afternoons. But, while leaving the Hôtel de Beaumont, and returning to town, she paid attention now to keeping the windows of the coach lowered. The horses made rapid progress over the pavement, and curious spectators could only make out the whitened head of the old woman dressed in subdued brown colors.

"Madame Fraque has renounced Satan, his pomp, and his works. – M. Fraque has grown younger by as many years as his wife has grown older," etc., etc.

The phrases varied! but the public curiosity did not dig any deeper. The episode with Firmin had not gotten out. The world, forgetting undoubtedly her who had just renounced it, did not ask whither she was able to direct her activities, that lively, hateful, stubborn woman; what drama had shaken and modified that little being; what could have become of so much stale vanity, so much coquetry and soured gallantry.

However, among the usual clichés about Madame Fraque, one variant all of a sudden appeared:

"Madame Fraque has been converted!"

Towards nightfall, one day of Lent, before the gaslight was lit, in the cold and sad hour when Noirfond's bells sounded the benediction lamentably, with her veiled face, in her hazelnut shawl, shriveled like a dead leaf, she had been seen alone, in the street, grazing the walls. And the bitter north wind that blew had appeared to push her just under the porch of a church.

An waft of incense penetrated her suddenly. It was "a salvation." The organ played mellowly, with melodious shivers that seemed to mourn tender feelings for the earth; then, the same motifs were taken up again by celestial voices, withdrawn unto incommensurable heights, which seemed to quiver with a divine love. Many of the women, kneeling, hid their face in their hands in such a way that one could not tell anymore whether they were old or young. Madame Fraque, she also, bowed down, with her mechanical fervor of before, – as on her bench, in the chapel of the convent, when she knew nothing yet of this world that she needed now to renounce. Imagining to herself that nothing had changed, that this "before" lasted forever, she mutter all the prayers of the rosary which she had not forgotten. When she thought about exiting, the organ was no longer playing, for a long time, and the church was somber and deserted. After a last "*Je vous salue, Marie,*" Madame Fraque withdrew from this first bath of piety, her heart less cold, comforted, entirely touched.

Two days later, she confessed. She took communion the following week. After that, her husband could not recognize her anymore. Religion, like a

marvelous spring of Youth, seemed to rejuvenate
Zoé. An interior satisfaction that was reflected in her
face, a rested and natural taint, with more harmony in
her bearing, made her positively less ugly. Her husband could not get over his surprise, when Zoé
changed brusquely her manner of living, retiring at a
decent hour in the evening and rising in the morning,
breakfasting and dining at the dining room table, with
her husband, at the exact hour. She conversed with
him, now, of this and that, without bitterness. If M.
Fraque didn't hear something, she leaned towards her
husband's "good ear" and, more distinctly, gracious-
ly, she repeated her phrase. She poured him something to drink from time to time. She even cut the
bread for him.

Touched, not wishing to be outdone by her
friendly conduct, Hector placed delicately, one
evening, under Zoé's napkin evidence of three settled
accounts, that of the jeweler, the milliner, and the
draper; three old debts, going back several years, several thousand francs each. In this epoch of conjugal
truce and appeasement, this husband brought to his
wife bouquets and gifts even. He had the delicacy of
not choosing rings, earrings, bracelets, toys which his
wife had nothing more to do with, which could have
awakened regrets. But, ingenious in seeking to please
her, and knowing Zoé's recent great devotion, he offered her a diamond cross, a rich book of hours, an
admirable Christ in ivory, a silk- and velours-padded
prie-dieu. It was a sort of late and pale, melancholic
honeymoon. M. Fraque had come to see himself suddenly at the end of his public career. The coup d'état
had dissolved the national guard, and the brilliant

lieutenant-colonel uniform was henceforth destined to fade at the back of a wardrobe. Not wishing to serve "a regime that had made the arrest of M. Thiers," M. Fraque submitted his resignation to the new minister of justice. The tacit simulacrum of conjugal reconciliation softened, at least for the ex-magistrate, the bitterness of no longer being somebody.

Chapter 8

At the time of her sudden conversion, Madame Fraque, feeling obliged to make a rather loaded general confession, full of those details that it pains a women to specify, had gone one afternoon to the miserable chapel at the convent des Capucins, located outside Noirfond, at the end of an out-of-the-way and solitary walk shaded by old elm trees. Before the single confessional, four old women, shaking their head, crippled by old age, who had dragged themselves there from the neighboring hospice des Incurables, were waiting their turn. In less than a quarter of an hour, father Pamphile had expedited them. Then, it was Madame Fraque's turn and the operation had never taken so much time before. Father Pamphile, a rough holy man with an unkempt and dirty grey beard, in a greasy homespun frock, came immediately to the point, called things by their true name, without periphrases, took no more than ten minutes to sweep out *grosso modo* this conscience smeared over by thirty years of adultery. Madame Fraque left the confessional feeling the nausea of a little mistress. It was good for a time, this rustic, this director of old poor women, who didn't smell of *eau de Cologne*! But her friend the baroness de Latour, who was well versed in these matters, would recommended to her a more suitable confessor... She had consulted the baroness, and the little abbé de la Môle became Madame Fraque's ordinary confessor.

He smelled good that one, always freshly shaven, with his curled, pomaded hair. The face pow-

der that he was in the habit of daubing his cheeks
with, after having washed, was always poorly removed. When he took out his handkerchief, an odor-
ous cloud of lavender perfume surrounded him. He
was a Breton, said to descend from an old family, and
hadn't but twenty-eight years of age. Several months
before, important recommendations had caused the
young priest to come to the diocese, in the capacity of
a secretary to the bishop. But M. de la Môle, not having pleased Monseigneur, had fallen into a demi-dis-
grace. He was offered a village curacy. Wishing at all
costs to stay in Noirfond, he said mass and confessed
at Saint-Jean, the aristocratic parish, as a simple, un-
attached priest.

Madame Fraque was immediately enchanted
by the young director. If all priests had been like "Father Pamphile," she would have given up on religion
probably, like an indelicate thing, repulsive, almost
cynical, good for the populace. She would have preferred to devote herself to *bezique*[8] like old Madame
Gombaud, or to the raising of spaniels. But, with this
tactful, penetrating gentleman who had a light touch,
a first confession seemed to her an hour of ordinary
conversation, of charming intimacy. Kneeling at the
back of that confessional with the opening covered by
a green curtain, she felt a little as if she were in her
boudoir. What a lofty and surprising perspicacious
doctor of souls was this pale and poetic child, whom
she saw, through the wire mesh, pushing back with
each instant the long curls of hair in order to look at
the sky. That one there could not fail to go far and

---

[8]*bezique*: a card game.

high! While receiving absolution from him, this old woman who had never been very romantic, already saw her new director as bishop, archbishop, cardinal, – always promising herself to come back often.

And she came back, developing more and more of a taste for religion and for her confessor. She no longer felt her existence to be empty as she had previously. Something absorbing, profound, had taken the place of that profane and always superficial agitation that swept her life away formerly, and which made the weeks, months, and years pass by so rapidly for her. As for her husband himself, without stopping, fundamentally, to hate him, she no longer dedicated all her free time, as before, to making every hour of his life difficult. Her claws, snapped off on the day she had realized her old age, remained buried in the flesh she had torn. While waiting for other claws to grow back in their place, she indifferently let Hector taste the false joys of an apparent rapprochement. Besides, she didn't even have the time any more to occupy herself with him, since the abbé de la Môle had said to his penitent:

– Madame, one must do good works...

She did them docilely, an innumerable amount of them. She gave to the box for the poor, to prisons, to the hospital, to the funds of Saint-Pierre, to the orphanage of Providence, to the Incurables, to the asylum for Abandoned Children, etc., etc. All the convents, all the collections, all the pious works of the city or diocese, had their share of the first liberalities of this repentant sinner. She gave even 500 francs for the chapel bell of the new small seminary. Mgr.

Matheron who had his heart set on the construction of
his seminary, which he wanted to make the glory of
his episcopate, took the sum from the hands of M. de
la   Môle, at one of his Sunday evening receptions.
The donor remained anonymous; Mgr. Matheron had
the proof that his ex-secretary was more useful at
Noirfond than in an out-of-the-way curate. Father
Pamphile, himself, after Madame Fraque's general
confession, had only thought of prescribing to her as
penitence a certain number of Hail Mary's and recita-
tions of the rosary "in the middle of the night, and
kneeling on the parquet." The abbé de la Môle, who
was not in favor of "uselessly mortifying penitences,"
preferred to recommend an alms, some gift agreeable
to God. Like a doctor who modifies his prescriptions
with each visit according to the phases of the disease,
after each confession, he counseled a new good work.

"It's not necessary to give a lot," he repeated
each time to Zoé, "but one must give with discern-
ment, and one must always give. A good work is an
effective and useful prayer, a prayer that has assumed
a body like Our Lord Jesus Christ, and which redeems
our faults without ceasing to be a prayer, just as our
divine Master redeemed our souls without ceasing to
be a God..."

She listened religiously to these subtleties,
without trying to understand them, already disposed
to believing with eyes closed everything that came
out of that mouth with the pure and thin lips. She felt,
what's more, completely transformed. Things she had
found most exorbitant, became easy and natural for
her. She who, formerly, had difficulty getting out of

bed at two o'clock in the afternoon, and whom one
saw only at a distance, only on important feast days,
to be present at noon mass, long after the first gospel;
every morning now, at seven o'clock, she ran to Saint-Jean to hear mass performed by the abbé de la Môle.
Her charitable zeal had limited itself previously to ac-
cepting a position of vice-presidency on the council
of women patrons engaged in charitable work for
nurseries. Once each Lent, for the concert, Madame
Fraque donated several banknotes. Then, at the theater, on the evening of the performance, Madame
Fraque, dressed to the nines, on the arm of some substitute Crown prosecutor wearing the commissioner's
rosette, preceded by the first president, followed by
Madame de la Tour and the mayoress, crossed, during
the interlude, the numbered chairs. And these four
high-society ladies arrived with great *frou-frou* in the
narrow artists' foyer to congratulate, in the name of
charity, the women singers, under the lorgnette of the
commissioners – a complete squadron in butter-
cup-yellow gloves – who squeezed in at the door and
laughed slyly. Now this Madame Fraque felt ready
for entirely other zeals, for modest charities, for
works meritorious in a different way, which she kept
to herself, her confessor and God.

     She found it even too gentle, too easy, this
first religious treatment that her prudent director ad-
ministered to her but in small doses. What did it cost
her to give several forty francs a week, she who had
never known the value of money! Her last lavish
worldly debts were settled, she didn't waste any more
money or time on her toilette, and still collected regu-
larly the ten thousand francs of rent from her dowry.

She realized economies now, therefore, all the while preserving her health. Religion was far from becoming for her as costly as fashion. She would have wanted, on the contrary, in the zeal of a new convert, to become devoted, to pay with her person, to accomplish great sacrifices. She got to the point of dreaming of unlimited devotions, she was thirsty to give herself, entirely, once and for all. She came to the point of finding them insignificant and pitiful, these first little sacrifices of money. Any more, she considered them like pure childishness pleasing to the abbé de la Môle, that she gave to him like a weak mother. But she felt stirring in her something other than maternity and she expected better.

Chapter 9

In those days, M. Fraque had experienced new inqui-
etudes: this time a subdued anguish, a malaise without precise cause, the vague apprehension of an approaching, unknown danger. One moment, he as-
cribed his troubles to a simple morose disposition, the
effect of coming old age, of idleness. He returned to
his pigs, went often to "*Villa-Poorcels*," made repairs
and embellishments. His wife refused to spend the
coming spring with him in the country; he went there
alone. But, the day after he arrived, boredom seized
him in the midst of his pigs. Why, again, had he resigned his position as magistrate? … Oh! that inop-
portune coup d'état!... If Noirfond had been now in
the process of holding elections, he would have immediately submitted his candidature for the opposi-
tion, so strongly did he feel the need to be shaken, to
distract himself. Then he felt completely surprised at
not having thought earlier about some grand voyage:
– Nice, Genoa, Florence, Rome, Naples, Venice; – after Italy, Switzerland, and the banks of the Rhine; –
finally Paris, which since 1829 ought to have changed
quite a bit, even though "Paris is always Paris," where
he would discover old friends again and memories of
his youth. Returned that same day to Hôtel de Beaumont, he had Isnard pack his trunks. Zoé was no more
disposed to accompanying him on a voyage than to
the countryside. In the evening, Hector took leave of
his wife who, distracted, received grudgingly, on her
stern yellow face, the traveler's goodbye caress. Towards ten o'clock, with heavy heart, he boarded the

diligence for Toulon. The following evening, M. Fraque had returned. In the diligence coupe, although alone, he had been unable to sleep. At Toulon, he hadn't even taken a look at the harbor: he had only visited the penal colony, where the sight of the convicts in green caps, condemned to drag their ball in perpetuity, had distressed the ex-Crown solicitor. He didn't have the courage to go any further, and his grand voyage was all of a sudden terminated.

So, there was nothing to do: no pretext of idleness, no distractions he could hope to find. M. Fraque became profoundly miserable again.

And it was neither old age nor inactive ambition that bothered him: but, his wife, always his wife! He didn't know why any more. He had opened his eyes wide: there was no Firmin to be found. He sensed however some new enemy, mysterious and invisible.

All of a sudden, one evening, at the bishop's palace, M. Fraque, who since the inauguration of his pigsty had maintained relations with Mgr Matheron, learned from His Greatness that one young priest, M. de la Môle, had just put on a firm footing the "Holy-Adolescence Children's Home."

The little abbot had purchased it and had it built.

"Where did he find so much money, my ex-secretary?" sighed the Monseigneur, who, himself, had all the difficulties in the world trying to complete his Petit-Seminaire, begun twelve years ago.

Then M. Fraque heard shouted in his ear:

"He's Madame's director!"...

This time, the husband did not receive the blow with cool composure, with his old presence of mind. His face reddened visibly; he took leave of Monseigneur very quickly. One minute later, while descending the great staircase of honor at the episcopal palace, M. Fraque tapped marble banister with his cane and said out loud to himself:

"I liked the scraps better."

Chapter 10

"Hup! Miss Jenny! hup! hup! hup!..."

And, at each instant, in a foul mood that day, M. Fraque's crop struck dryly on the croup of his mount.

It was always "Miss Jenny," but not the same as the old one, the first one, the one to whom Isnard had given so many pieces of sugar. That one, for a long time now, M. Fraque had had the sorrow of losing. And the years had marched on since then. So much so that the new Miss Jenny had become old in turn, very old, and, despite the oats and the pieces of sugar, of an apocalyptic thinness. The good beast, however, as if she felt that the disagreeable thoughts of her master should be shaken, pretended to gallop, which procured from the rider the diversion of tightening his knees, displaying his talents as a consummate rider. Almost standing in the stirrups, drawing in the reins, arching his back, with attentive eye, his hair standing on edge, M. Fraque, having become young again, passed quickly enough along the pavement of the exterior boulevard.

It was one o'clock. The wet nurses were giving milk to their kids, sitting on the old stone benches where the rain had over the years dug large holes. Against the ruins of Noirfond's rampart, covered with ivy, the nannies let their children run in the winter sunlight. All the nannies and wet nurses having turned around at the sound of the exceptional gallop of Jenny, smiled, saying to themselves:

"It's that eccentric M. Fraque passing by."

That frantic pace lasted only a while. On the main road to Marseille, Jenny resumed her peaceful, ordinary pace; and, relaxing the reins, his back still straight, but furrowing his brow and aged by twenty years, M. Fraque resumed his somber thoughts. On leaving Noirfond, the road to Marseille makes a great descent for nearly three kilometers. It hadn't rained for many days, and the mistral, that scourge of Provence, wasn't blowing. On that beautiful January afternoon, the road stretched white and clean before him, beneath the blue sky, bordered by its double row of young plane trees, all of them having conserved some tuft of rusty leaves that a bright sun made resplendent. The songs of birds emerged from both sides of the road in the country bathed in sunshine. There was even some brightness and joy along the yellow telegraph poles, up until the pile of symmetrical stones placed here and there. But M. Fraque's glazed-over eyes were fixed on the black mane of Miss Jenny.

He encountered lots of people. The laundresses, their parcels of linen on their head, were going to wash in the river that passes below the descent. The rentiers, old fellows in retirement, digested in the sun. Carters, coming from Marseille, climbed the ascent on foot. And, as that day was a Thursday, at each instant, students were seen passing, on a walk: the college, older and younger seminaries, many young girl pensioners. Everyone knew M. Fraque, the carters from Marseille as well as the bourgeois of Noirfond, the students paid to supervise children as well as the female instructors, the priests as well as the laymen, the old as well as the young. The men greeted him. The schoolboys threw familiarly little stones into Jenny's sabots. And everywhere, on the route to Marseille as on the long exterior boulevard, was a trail of dust, – the same smile on every mouth said:

"It's that eccentric M. Fraque passing by."

At about the middle of the descent, Jenny turned her ears suddenly: in the distance, something black was moving. But the prudent beast was reassured soon enough. Doctor Boisvert's uncovered vehicle was climbing the ascent, shaking its old, dilapidated cover[9] so much so that it also seemed to greet Mr. Fraque. The doctor, who was returning from a visit to a rural patient, conducted the vehicle himself, while reading his *Figaro*. He was already drawing the bridle to come to a halt in the middle of the road and to chat several moments with his client. But, in his preoccupation, M. Fraque spurred the belly of Jenny and trotted on past, in front of the practitioner, without noticing him.

At the bottom of the descent, once they had arrived at the viaduct with two arches that let the stream pass, a difference of opinion arose suddenly between Miss Jenny and her master. M. Fraque, wanting to take the towpath, pulled in vain on the reins in the direction of the mill; the old stubborn horse could not resolve to quit the road to Marseille, which was also that of *Villa-Poorcels*. The rider flew into a rage of blows with his spurs and riding crop. The mount

---

[9]Presumably folded back.

turned on herself, neighing with pain. In the end, but against her wishes, and dragging her hooves, Miss Jenny turned to the left, descended before the mill where men were loading a cart with sacks of flour, and took the towpath.

The bridge and the mill, left behind, disappeared slowing behind the trees. The great descent of the road to Marseille was soon nothing more than the end of a white ribbon hanging from the horizon. The towpath ran along the bank, where the sloping prairies terminated at the river. It was less a path than a trail where Jenny's sabots disappeared sometimes in the weeds. Below, in a bed too wide for her, the little river water bypassed the pink rocks, then dispersed over large stretches of sand that it didn't recover from save as a trickle in the broad silver meshes.

He passed nobody. During the summer, everyone from Noirfond comes to bathe in the river. There's shouting, singing, great outbursts of laughter at the water's surface. On each rock, groups of naked children, men in swimming trunks, women in bathing costumes, dry in the sun. During the winter, one finds only the laundresses crouching down in their plank boxes.[10] And here and there, some fisherman with his line out, eternally immobile, seemed to be part of the bank where he sat. Jenny proceeded slower and slower. M. Fraque had relaxed the reins; and, with his head weighed down by somber thoughts, he ended up by letting it fall forward, such that his chin now rested

[10]Plank boxes: women washing their clothes at the riverside would often use a three-sided box to sit in (four sides if you count the bottom of the "box"), so as not to get the clothes they were wearing wet or dirty.

on his shirt's white plastron. The sun bathed his face, making his strange profile stand out, shining on his long snow-colored hair. His long crop, held under his arm, seemed like some pike inclining its tip towards the ground. He could have been mistaken for an overwhelmed Don Quixote, fallen asleep on Rocinante.[11]

The small valley became enclosed, more solitary still. From time to time, bunches of tall trees stood out against the azure, – were reflected in the river. The laundresses' beaters could no longer be heard. To the right, a long, bare and rocky hill rose like a wall. And, on the Noirfond side, to the left, above the large prairies, were hills covered with olive trees, in the middle of which could be seen the rooves of several distant farmhouses. Thinking he was quite alone, M. Fraque began to sigh deeply.

He had arrived at "the Silver-Fountain." A barrier of rocks cuts across the bed of the river; the water, held back, flows in a sheet, gently. It is a thin sheet of limpid silver, on which the sun reflects, and which finishes with a little foam. Jenny wanted a drink. She took it upon herself to descend to the river's edge, and took several steps on the wet gravel. Her sabots sank in. But the rider let her go. His thoughts were far away. At the moment when Jenny, neck lowered, sniffed with avidity the mist of water from the Silver Fountain, M. Fraque lifted his head: big tears moistened his cheeks. The skinny mare continued drinking.

Suddenly, M. Fraque blew his nose four or

---

[11]Rocinante: Don Quixote's horse.

five times in a row, with a force that was loud enough to be heard a kilometer away. After that, he was another man, as if he had just stuffed his emotions into his pocket, with his handkerchief.

"Good animal! good animal!" he said, while patting affectionately Jenny's neck, as she continued to drink.

Cheered up now, Jenny trotted along the towpath, between two deep ruts dug out by the wheels of carts. The overwhelmed Don Quixote had woken up, and, while hopping along on Rocinante's back, whistled a hunting song, brandished his riding crop in the air, as if he had lashed a face. For several instants, in the sudden widening of the small valley, the main route d'Italie cut across the horizon in a big white line on a steep slope straight to the river. On the climb up from the towpath to the new viaduct, Miss Jenny didn't have the leisure to resume the playacting she had performed on the road to Marseille: her master spurred her into full gallop on the ascent that leads to Noirfond.

It was four o'clock. The sun shined now only on the upper floors of houses along the avenue d'Italie. On the benches, soldiers waited for the meal hour to return to the nearby barracks. The kids, with arms extended to keep their balance, walked along the thick beams in front of a chapel under construction. Trowel in hand, the masons worked on their scaffolds, at the same time that a manual laborer mixed lime in the middle of a large circle of sand. The noise from the stone cutters' chisels was continuous, grating.

A group of twenty small boys in blue uniform returned from a walk, two by two, the smaller ones first, followed by a young priest. They entered the house adjoining the chapel under construction by a door surmounted by a small cross, and with these words on it: "*Holy-Adolescence Children's Home*." Before following his pupils inside, the young priest remained one instant on the sill, looked all down the avenue, up to the entrance of the road to Toulon. Pale and thin, holding his head proudly, draped in an immense coat, his long curled hair falling onto his shoulders, coiffed with a wide, felt, high and pointed hat with only one side turned up, he could have been taken for a little Black Musketeer.[12] He went inside immediately and closed the door, precipitously. M. Fraque, appearing at the top of the ascent, emerged at full gallop onto avenue d'Italie.

Overworked, panting, her mane standing on end, the old mare passed with her head spinning before the benches where the soldiers were seated, in amazement, all of them, at this old man whom they saw every afternoon execute this fantastic cavalry charge. Miss Jenny was almost at once in front of the *Holy-Adolescence Children's Home*. Once there, as usual, she was made to stop short. And as he did everyday, his eyes sticking out of his head, menacing the chapel in construction with his riding crop, M. Fraque shouted out to the first passerby:

"Look at them building this dump!... It's with

---

[12]Black Musketeer: a member of one of two companies of musketeers, formed in 1664, the other company being the Grey Musketeers.

my money...!"

The phrase never varied. Each time M. Fraque threw it out to whomsoever it might be: bourgeois, worker, peasant, old woman, a young female laborer. Sometimes it was to an eight-year-old little child. On that day, M. Menu, a Protestant pastor, who was walking with a book in hand, received the phrase.

Chapter 11

M. Menu greeted the ex-Crown prosecutor with great respect, but with serious dignity. Then he continued his walk, by small paces, always holding his book open. But he wasn't reading any longer. M. Menu was reflecting.

In the evening, at the table, between his wife and his only son Eudoxe, the Protestant pastor spoke few words. While carving the chicken, his knife, hesitating, could no longer find the joints. Madame Menu, a small, chubby woman, with a very big fat face, daughter of a Genevan watchmaker, who had made some poor business decisions, finally removed the plate from her husband's hands.

After the meal, the two spouses, seated in a corner of the fireplace in their room with two beds, were no longer conversing. Madame Menu knitted. Monsieur turned over and over again the *Journal de Genève*. Eudoxe, an extern at college, was completing his work in the light of the petrol lamp. But, when their son wished them a goodnight, once abed and the lamp extinguished, M. Menu began speaking with his wife. An animated conversation was established, from one bed to the other, and was prolonged well into the night.

The following day, at the same hour, and as if by chance, M. Menu directed his walk before dinner toward avenue d'Italie. But the Protestant pastor, in appearance absorbed in reading the Gospel, it did not matter how many times he passed and repassed before t h e *Holy-Adolescence Children's Home*: suffering that day from a fit of gout, M. Fraque hadn't mounted his horse.

M. Menu would have better chances on the days that followed. He enjoyed many times the satisfaction of exchanging a tip of the hat with Mademoiselle de Grandval's husband. He even tried, from the sidewalk's edge, to engage in conversation with the rider. But it was necessary to shout loudly: the deaf man heard poorly, responded the wrong way, and the passersby turned their head. Losing hope that he could thus catch the old man in a day of communicative expansion, M. Menu ended up by taking his walks elsewhere, but a fixed idea, that he held onto for quite some time afterwards, didn't abandon him. And, at night, in the conjugal chamber, while next door, Eudoxe, his composition completed, snored like one of the blessed in heaven in his collegian's small room, it was long insomnias and all sorts of laborious schemes whispered from one bed to the other.

Winter finished thus. And, once again, summer succeeded spring. What the Menus, hidden away in the dark, lay in wait for with so much perseverance, "an occasion," never presented itself. The period of holidays was approaching. The end-of-the-year triple compositions, at college, had already begun. And, as all classes wrote these compositions from seven o'clock in the morning to noon, two times per week, on Tuesday and Friday, the Protestant pastor entered Eudoxe's room in his slippers, on those days. Often, the lazy boy went back to sleep again. At the end of a quarter of an hour, his father entered the room again, and, this time, removing the blankets, threw water on his face.

One Tuesday in July, M. Menu came to Eudoxe much earlier in the morning. Five o'clock had not yet sounded. Already dressed as if ready to go to church, the Protestant pastor sat down solemnly beside his son's bed. Paler than usual, he clearly had not slept the night before. Behind him entered Madame Menu, her hair already correctly coiffed, also wan in complexion, her face swollen, her eyes glazed with cold obstinacy. Eudoxe, still half-asleep, rubbed his nose, not fully aware what the matter was.

"Your mother and I," said the Protestant pastor, "we come to ask a favor of you... It's imperative that you receive something at the award ceremony."

Eudoxe remained very surprised. In third place, at the college of Noirfond, he passed for a dunce. His insolence, his slovenly attitude, his phenomenal laziness, had made M. Charboneau, the professor, prejudiced against him. He came to class with irreproachable homework, which his father had the weakness to do for him each day, that the son limited himself to copying mechanically. But he never bothered to learn the lesson, to follow an explication of the authors. Once in a long while, when a French essay assignment suited him, when a text of Latin translation seemed to him like an amusing puzzle to solve, Eudoxe wrote, and obtained, an honorable grade just like anyone else.

"But papa," he responded mischievously, "how do you expect me to obtain anything, this year, with M. Charboneau, who holds it against me that I'm not a Catholic, because I'm your son? Last year, it wasn't M. Charboneau, and I received the first-place certificate of merit in calculus."

"It's not a certificate of merit that you must obtain," shouted M. Menu, "but a prize!... Are you listening to me? a first- or second-place prize!... Those who obtain a certificate of merit sit on their bench, return home with their hands empty, while we want to see you mount the platform... It is absolutely necessary that you are crowned..."

Eudoxe struggled for a long time, in his bed. They had waited too long to inform him. All the compositions in the "disciplines" where he could have had a shadow of a chance, had already been completed, and he admitted to not having been fortunate. All that remained was the Greek composition, the Greek translation and Latin verses! The rascal even made a derisory proposition.

He was small like his mother, alert and supple like a monkey, with the same darting grimacing look on his face. He missed being able to take lunches at school any more, since M. Menu, in order to become his tutor, had decided that he would only take classes. It was so entertaining in the large courtyard shaded by plane trees, around the pool of water, everyone together; and his studies themselves, with the pleasant rounds of checker, the dirty conversations whispered behind piles of dictionaries, and the pipes smoked under the desk. Eudoxe maintained, then, before his parents that, if he was allowed to take school lunches again, he could still obtain a prize for gymnastics. At this moment, Madame Menu, who had not yet opened her mouth, took her turn speaking.

Better than her husband, she immediately made Eudoxe see the importance and the greatness of their projects constructed on an impending crowning achievement in public. She was his mother above all! The superhuman effort, the prodigious will, that she came to demand of her son, was after all in his own best interests and for his future even. Then, when she had exhausted her phrases, the practical woman bent on employing all means, and knowing well the soft spots of him whom she had brought forth from her bowels, added:

"For the composition that you must recite, which you mentioned, you have three weeks to pre-pare; and you have an excellent memory... We will help you, your father and I, to make you repeat it night and day; you won't do anything else. Myself, if necessary, I will learn it with you, all of it: *Athalie,*[13] the *Petit Carême*, [14] even the *Géorgiques*[15] and your *Jardin des racines grecques.*[16] "Finally" (and here she looked at him straight in the eyes), "from today for-ward, you may ask us for whatever you want..."

---

[13]*Athalie*: a play by Jean Racine.

[14]*Petit Carême*: literally "The Little Lent," a sermon written by Jean-Baptiste Massillon.

[15]*Géorgiques*: pastoral poems by Virgil.

[16]*Jardin des racines grecques*: literally "Garden of Greek radicals". A book that contained all the Greek radicals or roots, usually in verse form (to make them easier to remember).

The son jumped out of bed, smiling with mis-
chievous joy. While getting dressed, he already im-
posed conditions. For breakfast, he wanted *racahout
au lait*,[17] with toasted bread and butter. Until the day
of recitation, he would not go back to school: his father would write a sick note for him. He consented to
spend the greater part of the day memorizing the
prose and verse; but he would have his evenings free,
would leave by himself after dinner, would return towards midnight with a master key, "as if he was a student again." Finally, and above all, they would give
him some money.

Three weeks later, on Tuesday, the day of the
recitation, Eudoxe arrived at college at ten minutes to
seven in the morning, smoking a cigarette, a walking
stick under his arm, his hands in his pockets. To the
great astonishment of M. Charboneau and all the
class, he uttered what destiny designated, French,
Latin, Greek, without a single fault, without one hesitation, without a simple inversion of words. He was
first, and not having obtained any points from the
simple compositions, he still obtained second place.
At the end of the following week, the solemn distribution of prizes was held; Madame Menu was contented
with sending her husband to the ceremony and sto-
ically passed the afternoon at home, making apricot
jam.

M. Menu, dressed in black, stern and buttoned
more than usual, pale like his white tie, arrived early
in the large courtyard decorated with hangings and

---

[17]*racahout au lait:* a kind of chocolate milk, made from cocoa and
acorns, potato starch, etc.

garlands of laurel. His gaze, full of anxiety that day, were fixed on the red armchairs placed for notable personages in the front row, before the stadium sur- mounted by a long table holding the gilt-covered books and crowns. Already the boarders, in uniform, occupied their benches on each side of the stadium, a little bit back. The students continued to arrive, in light-colored trousers, their hair curled. Eudoxe was there, surrounded by a group of larger students in the midst of which his small person was hidden. Already, rows of chairs were stocked with parents, the curious, emotional and well-dressed mothers, little girls dressed in white perched on a bar of the chair in order to discover their cousin or their brother. The crowd was such that many newly arrived could no longer find a place to sit. Fathers, off to the side, leafed furtively through the list of students who had placed. Alumni, having returned to revisit their past, wan- dered in the second courtyard; and one noticed them, grown fat and prosperous, with rounded belly, dream- ing for a spell, their nose in the air, before the trapeze and the parallel bars; while others, leaning over the edge of the pool where they had learned to swim, touched the bottom with the end of their cane, pulling out dead leaves. But, completely fixated on his idea, M. Menu didn't take his eyes off the row of red arm- chairs.

Two or three of them remained empty. Mgr Matheron, the abbé de la Môle, the imperial prosecu- tor who had succeeded M. Fraque, Doctor Boisvert, the magistrates of the court, superior officers of the garrison had already taken their places. All of the sud- den, they all rose. The town's music welcomed with a

quickened pace the arrival on the stadium of the professors in cap and robe, the mayor, with his scarf and
sword, president of the solemnity. When everyone
had sat back down, M. Menu saw with horror, in the
last reserved places, ladies who were unable to find
an empty seat. The customary discourse, read with
great volubility by the stout professor of history who
lisped, caused him interminable anguish. With each
page that a hasty hand turned over at each instant, he
seemed to see his hope, espied from a distance, and so
meticulously prepared, grow thinner and be reduced
to nothing. When the Principal rose in turn and had
begun with a vibrant voice: "Young pupils," the
Protestant pastor removed his hat and mopped his
forehead. At this moment, he lost all hope. It was finished: he whom he had expected, for one reason or
another, that year, was unable to attend. He had to
start all over again! He needed to make a decision,
find a new strategy, come up with a simpler, surer
scheme. Suddenly, while the discourse given by M.
the Principal was still being applauded, the Protestant
pastor had to lean against the trunk of the plane tree
near which he was standing: M. Fraque was in front
of the stadium, alarmed like someone who arrives
late, his white hair standing on end, receiving hand-
shakes, looking for a place to sit. Doctor Boisvert was
delighted to give him his, in order to leave ostensibly:
his personal enemy, M. the mayor, was already blowing his nose and lightly coughing in order to prepare a
clear voice.

The rest continued all on its own. The short
speech by M. the mayor seemed to M. Menu golden
music. When the vice-principal, who was announcing

the laureates, was at the third, and had called: "Recitation of the classics... second place: Eudoxe Menu, of Noirfond, a free student..." everything happened according to plan as drawn up one night in the conjugal chamber by the Menus, from one bed to the other. Eudoxe assumed his attitude, for form's sake, of looking about in the crowd; then he said softly in the ear of the master of studies who was waiting there, prize and crown in hand:

"Monsieur the ex-Crown prosecutor..."

M. Fraque loved youth; for him, palm leaves awarded for academic excellence had been a religion. He placed the crown as far down as the ears on the secondary-school student; then, as he was versed for some time in the study of phrenology and Gall's system,[18] he walked his hands quickly over the face of young Eudoxe "to feel the bumps," all the while addressing to him a "speech," that he concluded by kissing his cheeks.

The following day, M. Menu, Madame Menu and their son paid a visit to M. Fraque, under the pretext of thanking him. In addition, Madame Menu, the day before, had succeeded perfectly in the preparation of her apricot jam.

---

[18]Gall's system: after Franz Joseph Gall, the founding father of modern phrenology.

Chapter 12

In the large salon, painted by Boucher, before the Protestant pastor absorbed in religious attention, before the distracted Madame Menu who, from the corner of her housewife's eye, calculated the value of the panels and old furniture, M. Fraque, talkative that day and in a hospitable mood, returned to his phrenological observations.

"That boy there has the protuberance of a highly developed memory..."

He enlarged on the importance of that faculty of understanding: "Without the memory, where would the orator be, or the scholar, the magistrate, the military man, the man of letters?" and other phrases of discourse on the distribution of prizes, as if that of the day before had left resonances of ideas in his mind. Besides, M. Fraque had gotten to the point of living in a sort of somnambulism apart from anything that was not his *idée fixe* and secret torment. He rose every day, ate, read, left the house, returned, spoke, like the devil so to speak and out of habit. His deliberate eccentricity of former days had transformed into a natural strangeness, a mania, and bordered now on madness. Then, at the least shock, for a word, for nothing at all, on a simple association of ideas, the pained man still bled, deep down inside the automaton that he had become.

"There, hold on!" he said, and with his thumb he pressed against the boy's cerebellum; "the passionate instincts equally very developed..."

It was what made great criminals, when the passion was not balanced by the intelligence, nor moderated by reason. In the "child," M. Fraque noted this equilibrium. The "child" was therefore well suited to become somebody, and M. Fraque found himself entirely naturally compelled to draw up a sort of horoscope for him. At that moment only, he realized, and was made to see, that he knew nothing about the father or mother of the "recitation prize" winner whom he had crowned.

"Pardon me, Monsieur, not to have introduced myself earlier. I am M. Menu, pastor of the reformed Church..."

And as M. Fraque, not having heard well what he had said, used his hand to make an ear trumpet, M. Menu repeated in a strident voice:

"M. Menu, pastor of the reformed Church!"

It was a shock. M. Fraque, who two days before had seen the scaffolding of the chapel of the Holy-Adolescence removed, got up trembling. He walked to the window jerkily, looked for a moment through the glass at the foliage, grown red in autumn, of the mansion's beautiful chestnut trees. At the back of the salon, the Menus, pale with emotion, waited in silence.

Then, M. Fraque returned with slow steps, master of himself:

"Monsieur, the pastor, you do know that this evening you will dine with me, all three of you..."

Madame Menu excused herself, personally; and, at the wink of an eye by her husband, she took her leave and retired with her son Eudoxe. M. Menu, himself, stayed.

Such was the origin of the great intimacy between M. Fraque and the Menus. It quickly became the talk of the town of Noirfond. Doctor Boisvert went so far as to spread the news that M. Fraque, in little time, was expected, in hatred of his wife's devotion, to convert solemnly to Protestantism. In effect, M. Fraque never set foot again in the bishop's palace. M. Fraque dined several times a week at the Protestant pastor's house. At each instant of the day, Isnard went looking for the Menus on behalf of his master. Outside, one never encountered M. Fraque without some Menu at his side. At five o'clock, it was not rare to see M. Fraque out walking to and fro, in front of the gate of the college, waiting for the pupils to exit. The bell pealed finally. Eudoxe appeared, books under his arm, and flying into the arms of Mr. Fraque, as if he were his father or a rich uncle.

The Menus ended up by gaining a foothold at Hôtel de Beaumont. Eudoxe, now, came daily to do his homework in the small room in front of M. Fraque's office, on the same table where the young Firmin traced his arabesques with a quill formerly. Eudoxe had no hesitation either of inviting his comrades. These gentlemen, rhetoricians and philosophers, entered by the small gate, considered the garden as their own, raised a hullaballoo by their antics, – a completely troubling new life – under the old chestnut trees; and the smoke from their cigarettes made the stupefied statues nauseous maybe. M. Menu spent hours sometimes reading under an arbor, at the very back. Madame Menu came every afternoon. The concierge and Isnard having received their orders that she was allowed to go straight up to M. Fraque's office, without asking anyone, install herself in a window, and take out her work from a small varnished sack.

Finally, one evening, Doctor Boisvert said with everyone circled round him:

"You didn't hear, messieurs? M. Fraque has just had a close call... the beginning of a phthisis. I applied an efficacious vesicant just in time... Ah well, do you think you can guess who acted as his sick nurse?"

"The wife?" one man threw out with a little smile, who was playing a game of checkers with M. the mayor.

"Ah! well yes, the wife! If by that you mean the wife of the Protestant pastor... Madame Menu spent last night in the room of the sick man, on a leather divan... She's the one who took off the vesicant in front of me!... She's planning to spend this evening there as well..."

All these gentleman looked at each other.

M. the mayor himself, even though Doctor Boisvert was his personal enemy, allowed himself to be interrupted in the middle of his profound scheme to get a queen.

Then, Doctor Boisvert, happy, lowering his voice with a discretion that belied the sparkle in his eye:

"I profited from a minute when Madame Menu could not hear us, and I gave my patient some good counsel... I told him: 'You know, you are much older than Madame Menu, you! and also, you're not a woman... So, don't be imprudent. If you don't believe me, you will be screwed.'"

Chapter 13

Since the middle of summer, the construction of the chapel of the Holy-Adolescence had been finished. But the organ and the widows, ordered from Paris, had not arrived. The carpenter entrusted with delivering the pulpit and the confessional asked for a delay of six weeks, because of the sculptures. In spite of Madame Fraque's impatience, it was necessary to wait for the Feast of All Saints for the inauguration. Then, it became evident that it would never be ready before Christmas.

At the beginning of December, one afternoon, the abbé de la Môle showed up by carriage at the bishop's palace. Prostrated at the feet of Mgr Matheron, the young priest supplicated His Greatness to invoke the protections from on high over the nascent work of the Holy-Adolescence, by coming to bless it, by celebrating the first holy mass in the chapel. In three seconds, a violent battle ensued within Monseigneur: his incomplete seminary, the twelve hundred thousand additional francs asked for by the architect for new estimates, an inveterate antipathy with regards to M. de la Môle, so many temptations to send brutally packing his ancient secretary! But with a marvelous suppleness of Catholic diplomacy and as a man of the world, Monseigneur knew how to gain the upper hand over himself and immediately accepted with a smile.

"His Greatness will fix the day and the hour himself," added humbly the Breton priest.

"Wait," said Monseigneur while consulting the little nacreous notebook inlaid with silver; "I don't see anything possible but Christmas Eve,... Yes, Christmas Eve at ten o'clock precisely."

The abbé de la Môle had only three weeks for the last preparations. Madame Fraque and he didn't lose a single minute. Three mornings in succession, they took the six o'clock diligence to spend the day in Marseille, to visit the merchants of religious articles. He turned the shops upside down, wearing out the shop assistants, wishing to see everything, choosing like a man of taste and haggling, as if he were paying with his own money. She, sitting in the most obscure corner, approved everything with a nod of the head, watching only him, not taking her eyes off of him. But what delighted her the most was the meal she took with him in the middle of the day in the deserted dining hall of the *Hôtel du Vatican*, which has the speciality, in Marseille, of accommodating priests.

The *á la carte* service was very slow. They were made to wait indefinitely for a beefsteak with potatoes. There was little light coming in through the one window, which gave onto a narrow alley that led to rue Paradis. The noise of carriages could not be heard. The opaque white curtains, the dull tapestry, the yellowed ceiling, oozed a glacial peace of sacristy. On the tablecloths, hanging low with a rigidness of altar cloth, one would have sworn there was a chalice next to the cruet of oil and vinegar. And, while waiting for the waiter to serve them, she was there at the table with her God, silent, in adoration, taking communion under both species: by devouring him with her eyes and drinking in his breath. Sometimes, at the small narrow table, upon the chance light touch of his soutane against her knee, she nearly fainted.

On the evening of the third day, they took a *fiacre* to complete their purchases. When the hour of last departure of the diligence was approaching, she hazarded to say:

"We will never have the time to finish... In any case, what do you say, we could sleep here, at the hôtel?"

And she looked him straight in the eyes.

The abbé de la Môle's face darkened.

"No, you well know I cannot stay out all night."

And, sticking his head out the window:

"Quicker, driver, quicker!... There's a tip in it."

So she sat back into her corner, glum, sunken.

That evening, in the diligence coupe, she didn't open her mouth, for all the first half of the journey. Then, at a village relay, while new horses were being hitched up, she said to him suddenly:

"I want a copy of the key to the chapel... That, you cannot refuse me..."

The abbé shrugged his shoulders, then wrapped himself more comfortably in his coat in order to sleep.

Two days later, she obtained the key however. The locksmith's apprentice brought it to her towards fall of day, at the Hôtel de Beaumont. She dined, waited until nine o'clock; then, as it was pouring rain, she put on her clogs, grabbed an umbrella, threw a shawl over her shoulders. She arrived soaked in front of the Holy-Adolescence Children's Home, having stepped multiple times right in the middle of large puddles of water. The avenue d'Italie was deserted. With what beating of the heart she felt the key pene- trate the lock, and the door open on its well-greased hinges!

She had just closed it carefully behind her. The chapel was completely dark. She needed to sit down at first, and took several paces, while groping around. Her foot hit against something sonorous, an empty case left there. And she sat down, happy for having come, feeling good, not even remembering any more that she had, in her pocket, a candle and some matches.

She rested for a long time sitting. An odor of paint and new masonry seemed delicious to her. Now she could come whenever she wanted! At all hours, day and night, she would find herself in the middle of this atmosphere, which bathed her heart in a gentle warmth. The night especially was good. The dark- ness, didn't it feel to her like a light velvet coat flow- ing over her shoulders? She would sometimes wait until dawn when the stained glass in the great rosace above the altar turned blue. And she rose comforted, completely light on her feet.

She had just lit the candle. Muffling her steps,

she passed like a shadow among the other boxes that had not yet been unpacked, placed there on the straw, in the middle of the rubble. She walked around the altar. She raised the candle to examine the effect of the pulpit recently put in place. Then, she mounted the tribune.

She wanted to see everything, ascribing importance to every detail, full of meticulous solicitude, like a mother furnishing the first apartment of her son. The organ-harmonium, wrapped in a cover, was too far to the left; having found its correct place, she propped it up with small pieces of wood. A swivel stool would be needed, and a compartment for storing the music. Here, a painting would do well.

And, with her elbows on the balustrade, she asked herself whether anything had been forgotten in Marseille, what a surprise she could make him. The day when he had received from her the first thousand-franc bills for "The Home," she remembered him, what joy like a child! She wanted to see him again like that, shaking wildly his long curled hair. At that moment, she climbed back down and crossed again the length of the chapel to go, behind the altar, and open a small door, that of the sacristy.

It was locked by a bolt on the inside. She returned home towards midnight, terribly sad.

And, for two days, wishing to be strong, she didn't return to "The Home." But how many times did she find herself, hat on head, hand on doorknob! Once even, an afternoon, she went as far as the stairs, descended halfway down a floor. Then she had the courage to climb back up again and to put on her slippers and dressing gown. And she spent the evening wanting to write to him.

When she had sent away her chambermaid, who had come to revive the fire, she opened her blotter, chose a new quill, took a scented piece of paper with her initials on it. Then she removed from their case her reading glasses, which she affixed to the bridge of her nose, after having meticulously wiped the lenses. And with the same hand that had completed for M. Fraque a sepia drawing begun in the convent, she started writing: "Monsieur..." in large uppercase letters, hesitant, fearful; and that was all! She remained hours, quill in hand in the air before a blank page, her heart full and moved, but not daring.

Two days later, around noon, she was completely shaken up, when one of the young pupils of M. de la Môle came to inform her that she was needed, to finish decorating the chapel.

"I'll slip on a dress," she responded. "Tell him that I am coming."

She didn't even take the time to eat breakfast. She found the abbè de la Môle before the altar, mounted on a double ladder, his soutane raised with pins. It was a happy afternoon. She held the ladder. The abbè consulted with her from time to time. And she passed him the greenery and artificial flowers.

Finally, the great day had come. Madame Fraque, all in black like a widow, arrived well before the hour, and climbed immediately onto the tribune.

For over a week now she had chosen her place, a chair in a corner, turned to an angle to face the organ. She removed her gloves, kneeled, closed her eyes, hid in her hands her face: it appeared slender, had grown thinner, was a little yellow under the turned-back black crêpe veil.

The chapel was deserted. The new stained glass did not gleam with the grey sky of that lazy winter morning. Here and there, in the corners, large stretches of shadow hung, like the night, unswept. It was melancholic and dark, also, inside her. She didn't know anymore where she stood in life, nor what she had wanted before, nor what she was still expecting. And, in that great wellbeing of uncertainty of anything anymore, she forced herself to pray. She fretted to supplicate an unknown, but all-powerful, being to make something happen that she had no idea about.

The sacristy door opened. Someone coughed and walked. She unfolded her hands, saw that a pupil was lighting the candles; and, without thinking, she counted them as they were lit, the yellow, upright and pointed flames. Suddenly she closed her eyes again, angry with herself for this distraction as if it were a sacrilege. And she lost herself in a more profound fervor.

She no longer occupied herself with what went on below. However, the revolving door of the chapel at each instant opened and closed. The parents, on entering, gave their invitation card to the pupil posted there, looking for a good place. There was a commotion of chairs, a growing murmur of conversations. Ten o'clock sounded. A noisy and jerky stamp-

ing of feet came out of the sacristy, made a tour
around the altar, came to finish along the four benches reserved for the pupils of the Holy-Adolescence.
All of the sudden, she felt a warmth in her heart: she
hadn't heard him mount the tribune, her eyes had not
re-opened, but she knew he was there.

It was him alright. The abbé de la Môle
opened the organ, put some music on the pulpit,
raised the swivel stool by rotating it, then, once seated, pulled out the register of "celestial voices." At
that moment, she opened her eyes, and lifting her veil,
still kneeling, she wrapped him with her avid gaze,
the same gaze she employed during their meals together at the *Hôtel du Vatican*. However, Monseigneur had just made his entrance in episcopal
clothing, the intoxication of the incense mounted, the
organ played, in a waltz movement, the suave joy of
triumph. But she forgot everything. Nothing absorbed
her but the child's lanky waist divined under abbé de
la Môle's fluted surplice; what seemed to her
adorable was the little morsel of young, warm, downy
neck where she would have wanted to press her lips.
She didn't return to her senses until, the ceremony
ended, the abbé de la Môle closed the organ precipitously, in order to go into the sacristy and join Monseigneur.

At that moment she lowered her veil again,
and wanted to recommence praying. The chapel became deserted again. The candles were snuffed. The
parents had departed to lunch in haste, in order to return around three o'clock, for the theatrical represen-
tation. She remained petrified on her chair, not being

hungry, not noticing that the time passed. Then, she lifted herself like an automaton, descended the tribune, traversed the chapel, passed by the sacristy, and found herself in a long corridor that was poorly lit, without exposure to light except by the windows that looked over on the large study hall.

Seated on a small bench that she had taken from the sacristy, Madame Fraque held open a curtain. Through the vertical stripes of the glass, she saw only a maitre d', in costume, and several work hands clearing away the two large gala eating tables, offered by the abbé de la Môle to His Greatness, the several priests that had accompanied the bishop, and the twenty-four young men of the home.

"He's in the courtyard with Monseigneur!" she told herself with tender emotion. "He's showing him the elm, the water fountain that's working as of today, the climbing roses..."

And, as loud bursts of laughter from the children came to her down the corridor:

"He's making them try, in Monseigneur's presence, the velocipede from the *Bazar de Marseille*."

The work hands transformed hastily the study hall, previously an eating hall, into a theater hall: a plank raised for the scene, a curtain running along a rod for the backdrop, the benches and chairs of the chapel for sitting on by the public, who were beginning to arrive. Parents, ecclesiastics, ordinary invitees equipped with a pass, and Monseigneur himself had all taken their place already, while the blows of the workers' hammers continued to echo still. They were behind schedule. From time to time, the abbé de la Môle appeared, busy, but smiling and gracious, murmuring something to make Monseigneur patient, and disappeared behind the backdrop. The young actors were getting dressed in the abbé's room, whose lodging, which adjoined the scene, served for the wings.

Finally, three strikes. The curtain opened. Two pupils, in toga and buskins, declaimed verses on stage. Several more pupils entered and exited, and, guards rigged out with wooden swords, paper cuirasses, stood up straight, impassible. Behind the glass of the corridor, where she was stationed as if in a gated loge, Madame Fraque paid no attention to the tragedy.

"What is he doing now in his room?"

His room! He never wanted to let her see it, since the masons and the painters had worked on it some more. One entered it by that door painted white at the end of the corridor. She imagined it full of light and cheerfulness, with light-colored wallpaper printed with soft blue bouquets chosen by herself, and two wide windows opening onto the water fountain, onto the baskets of flowers in the small private garden. But she would have wanted to know the arrangement, to know where the wardrobe with a mirror was, and the bookcase and the bed, the bed particularly which she had wanted to be made of rosewood, tall, voluminous, bulky, but comfortable and wide like the bed of a young bride. Suddenly, in the middle of her revery, she shivered: a door at the end of the corridor opened and closed, a sound of footsteps, someone behind her... She turned around; already her two small hands, pale and withered, pressed a warm hand that was not retracted immediately.

"It's good, it's good," said the abbé de la Môle.

And he withdrew his hand gently. He added:

"It's going along very well, don't you think?... In spite of himself, Monseigneur's eyes are wide open, is pleasantly surprised by what he's seen... I'm content."

One of those smiles such as one does not have but several times in a lifetime, passed over Madame Fraque's face. He didn't go away. In order to raise the curtain so as to watch the tragedy, he leaned familiarly over her, pressing on her shoulder a little. She felt herself nearly in his arms, there, in the shadows, not daring to move, nor to open her mouth, for fear of abridging this moment. Then, next to them, in the hall, as the hero of the piece terminated a long tirade at the end of the act while raising his arms to the sky, unanimous applause sounded out. And the abbé de la Môle getting up, said:

"The last act lasts only several minutes. I have to go."

She couldn't help saying:

"Already!"

"Yes... I must ensure that the Monseigneur's crew has arrived."

She had suddenly the despair of watching him frown. He added with a strong tone.

"And you, if anyone found you here... Is this your place?... Get a move on... You should have guessed it would displease me."

She wanted to respond: her lips were quivering already; so many things came to her at the same moment! But the abbé de la Môle was no longer present. She looked for a last time at the white door at the end of the corridor. Then, resigned, she left, head lowered. She carried her small bench to return it, in passing, to the sacristy.

But, that evening, she couldn't resist. At eleven o'clock, she found herself passing out through the Hôtel de Beaumont's door, with her copy of the key to the chapel in her pocket. It was freezing, at several degrees below zero, in the streets of sleeping Noirfond. She didn't feel cold: underdressed, her hat, covered only by a fur-lined coat with the hood pulled back. She didn't take a simple detour that would have allowed her to avoid crossing the Promenade, and passed before the lit-up windows of a Circle. Several minutes later, she introduced herself into the deserted chapel, and went straight to the altar, groping her way among the chairs left in disorder since the ceremony that morning. This time, the bolt of the little door behind the altar was unlocked.

In the sacristy, she her courage began to fail her; she continued however to advance, more slowly, on the balls of her feet. But when she slipped into the corridor, there was a sudden glare: there, at the end, a bright light, from the half-opened door of the abbé's room...

She advanced closer, while pressing up against the wall, holding her breath. She saw into the room now, and, in the nook of the alcove, under the thick curtains, the bed was undone, and he, in slippers, reclining in a low armchair, reading an enormous book. A large bright flame danced in the fireplace. He turned a page. He was completely absorbed in his reading, very calm. In his face, where the lampshade projected all the brightness of the lamp, not a muscle budged. She placed her hands on her chest to reduce the beating of her heart.

"When he turns the page again," she told herself, "I'll enter."

Almost immediately the abbé de la Môle turned a second page. Then, with her face forward, closing her eyes without wanting to, she pushed the door open heroically.

He showed neither surprise nor anger. Very naturally, as if he were receiving an ordinary visit, he got up out of his chair, and pushed it in front of the fireplace for Madame Fraque. He remained standing, and waited.

She was a long time without saying anything. Her mouth was dry. And, with her two eyes drawn to the fire, she was struck with a great shiver. Why also wasn't he speaking? Why wasn't he rushing her as usual, this time when she felt ready to hear everything, when she had come to make an end of it? If he had only threatened to throw her out at the door: a slap, at least, would have pleased her! But this silence!... She had just pushed her chair near the fireplace, her hands touched the flame almost, and she was cold.

"You were waiting for me, then?" she said finally.

He sniggered without responding. And she was at the end of her courage. Now that she found herself there, alone with him, she felt foolish and empty. It was like before, as when she had wanted to write, and after having written "Monsieur..." she remained for hours with the quill in the air facing the blank page. Nevertheless, she got up and mechanically took several paces in the room. In front of the wardrobe with a mirror, she turned her head so as to avoid seeing herself. After having gone as far as the window with its closed shutters, standing now in front of the bookshelf, stupid, she considered the hole left by the large volume removed by the abbé to read, in the middle of the bindings lined up. Then she seemed interested in what was cluttering up the dresser-toilette: with the flasks of scents, the large sponge, the small ivory brushes, the deep washbasin where remained a little soapy water. Lastly another two paces, and she found herself at the entrance to the alcove, before the great new rosewood bed, pumping its mattresses, terracing the pillows, fluffing up its eiderdown comforter under a dais of fabric curtains falling low. The quilt had already been drawn back, the blanket ready. Invincibly attracted, Madame Fraque leaned forward into that tabernacular nook; and there, beside herself suddenly, intoxicated, she pressed her face against the sheet and covered it with kisses.

The abbé de la Môle grew very pale. For a instant, he lost his calm and self-possession. Standing before the fireplace, his hand on the back of a chair, which he had brought forward from the back of the room just in case, he remained there, turning his back to the alcove, not knowing whether he should sit down.

"Be reasonable, I beg you," he implored without turning round.

His arm trembled. He was afraid. His voice crawled, slow and cowardly:

"Come put yourself back in the chair... We'll talk... Here, come, I'm waiting for you."

She obeyed. But when he saw her there, near him, her hair ruffled, an extraordinary sparkle in her eyes, almost young, totally vibrating still with the fit of passion that had shaken him, but already docile and hanging on his lips, the abbé de la Môle regained his assurance gradually.

He was speaking now, and about himself, nothing but about himself, with a naif, total, and admirable egoism. His future above everything! something serious, important, venerable even; a sort of sacred mountain that existed there, in front, obstructing the horizon, and around which the rest of humanity groveled like dust. And ambitious projects, all sorts of small intertwined and tortuous paths to attain the summit of the mountain. All that mixed with emotional returns to his childhood, with phrases like this: "I already had the Faith!" with other great words: Duty, Prudence, Sin.

Under this shower, she shivered. Devouring him with her eyes and drinking in his breath, she was drawn near to him like a child who is cold. From one minute to the next, her love, chilled to the bone, began to shrivel. He was doubtless right! That pure mouth could not be wrong. She was crazy to have come, and above all, great God! to do what? It would be a sin to prevent him from going to sleep, this man, who had an eminent future ahead of him, who ought to be exhausted after a day like today. There was more of the mother in her now.

The abbé had just cleared his throat in the middle of a phrase. She got up.

"You've got a cough!" she said, addressing him familiarly for the first and the last time in her life. "I'm leaving; you should go to bed quickly..."

He didn't keep her. She opened the door. She turned to look one more time at the room, where she should never return. And she felt something of a weakness. Her legs buckled and her eyes grew moist. A last temptation: if she was only able to see him in bed, to wait for him to fall asleep, to remain there on tiptoes until he was tucked in under the covers. It was a supreme need of devotion, the thirst of a voluptuousness to spoil him and to be good. Then, an idea came into her head, just like that, all of a sudden. And with a resigned smile, she said:

"Tomorrow, at three o'clock, I will come to pick you up.... I won't say any more, it's a surprise..."

The abbé's face lit up. Then she left.

The following day, at three o'clock, Madame Fraque conducted the abbé to the notary and made her will by nominating him as her only heir.

Chapter 14

One afternoon, towards the end of winter, Madame Fraque died of pericarditis.

When the care person, a sister of Hope, had informed him that it was over, M. Fraque hardly entered the room of his wife. He hadn't yet digested the will, and, on top of that, he had just made, on his own side, in the presence of a notary, legacy of all his possessions to the Protestant pastor. He stayed for just one minute, standing beside the bed, eyes dry, to look for the last time at the woman who had empoisoned his existence; then he exited brusquely.

"Isnard, go prepare Miss Jenny!"

And, as the old domestic's eyes widened:

"I'm going to the countryside to do nothing," he added with irritated resolution. "Do you understand? nothing whatsoever... Idiot, this is the business of Madame's heirs..."

After his master had departed, Isnard, alone, having lost his head, ran, both to M. Menu, and to M. de la Môle. Without seeing each other, without consulting each other, these two ministers of enemy worship shared silently the job. The Catholic priest prepared a sumptuous religious burial for the following day. The Protestant pastor registered her death with the civil authority, also took it upon himself to draw up and send on behalf of the husband letters of announcement. Eudoxe, himself, wrote the addresses.

Upon arrival at the avenue of plane trees at *Villa-Poorcels*, Miss Jenni, having gone flat out, was covered in sweat. The rider handed the bridle to the first farmhand he came across, recommending that he prepare her dinner and make her bed. It was still day. M. Fraque wandered for a long time on the terrace and in the prairie, hands in pocket, forgetting to draw near his pigs. He didn't seem however grieved. He ate with appetite. In the evening, which he passed in his room in front of a large fire of vine shoots, he read for a moment the journal. And he fell asleep, very late it is true, telling himself that he was not sad, that he didn't wish to be, that his wife after all had been the fatality of his life; that without her a man of his merit would have achieved an entirely different career, would have written perhaps, acted, left something behind, been a second M. Thiers; finally that, his wife dead, he was going to be able at least to live a bit tranquilly, him, the old egoist.

On the morning of the following day, M. Fraque was finishing his breakfast when his farmer came to him to announce, with all sorts of embarrassed circumlocutions, a bad piece of news. Miss Jenny had fallen ill during the night. Her respiration hampered, she remained lying on her litter, refusing to eat the hay and oats, not having even touched her pieces of sugar. The farmer had wrapped her in blankets himself. A farmhand was already in route to seek out a veterinarian. To the great surprise of the farmer, who knew however from Isnard that their master "loved animals more than people and would rather lose a relative than a mare," M. Fraque received the news without flying into a rage.

"Ah!" he said while pouring himself something to drink, "I'll come to the stable in just a moment."

The farmer, finding Monsieur so well disposed to hearing annoying things, spoke to him also of a threat of swine epidemic, which had taken away four of the livestock in the last week.

"You will lead the veterinarian to the pigsty also."

And M. Fraque succeeded tranquilly to peal a pear. His dessert finished, he took up his hat and cane, and began, as the day before, to wander over the terrace and the prairie. Soon, the mare and the pigs, his dear beasts, definitively forgotten, he found himself on the main road without really knowing how he got there, probably by a great circuit through the vineyards and the plowed land. And, as if taken by a sudden need to walk, his legs, quasi-octogenarian, began walking all by themselves in the direction of Noirfond. From time to time, on a kilometric marker, he rested like a man who was not pressed. Once even, changing direction, he found himself back where he had started some time previously, to prove to himself that he had no goal, but that he was out walking quite simply to walk. But an impulse that he didn't want to acknowledge, pushed him once again towards the town.

He was already at the viaduct with two arches and the small river.

"Well! I have walked quite a bit!" he said, as

if coming out of a dream.

The steep incline was there before him. Some one hundred paces still, and he would see the trees along the Promenade.

"But I'm not going to Noirfond!" he shouted angrily.

And he launched himself very quickly to the right, on the towpath where, on a certain day, Miss Jenny had been forced to descend by kicks of the spurs and blows of the riding crop. He passed before the mill where men were again loading a cart with sacks of flour; he left behind the rich prairies sloping towards the pink rocks of the river, and did not see the laundresses crouching in their plank boxes, nor the fishermen with eternally immobile lines; he did not stop in that solitary valley hollow where his eyes, previously, had suddenly grown moist, while Miss Jenny plunged her nostrils into the milky foam of the *Silver Fountain*. He arrived under the second viaduct. He had merely to climb up onto the bridge, and, from the parapet itself, he would discover the beginning of the avenue d'Italie, and the large buildings pierced by the small windows of the barracks.

"No, I'm not going back to Noirfond!" he repeated with rage.

He passed, almost running, under the viaduct, and continued to climb back up the river. But after an instant, he had on his left, between Noirfond and himself, "Poorman's Hill": a large bare hill, without trees, without bushes. A sad grey mass of stones, cracked

here and there with the holes of ancient abandoned
quarries. M. Fraque knew it well, that hill. As a child,
once, his nanny had brought him walking this far;
then, seized suddenly with panic at the sight of a
ragged man, a marauder with a bad look on his face
from those American quarries of Noirfond, she had
picked him up in her arms and run as far as the gates
of the town. As a schoolboy, one day after they had
escaped by jumping over the schoolyard wall, they
came here as a group of boys to get tipsy for a whole
afternoon on pure air, laughter, cries, liquorice water
shaken up in a bottle; and they played at cops and
robbers, and they skipped stones, and they descended
sheer slopes by sliding down on their backside; all
that until night, until the terrible return to Hôtel de
Beaumont, when the first president, his father, had
sent him to bed without dinner. Later as a young man,
a rifle on his shoulder and a book in his hand, he had
hunted on that hill. Later, finally, much later, in a
colonel's gold brocaded uniform, he had come here to
drill the Republican national guard. Also, after a moment, M. Fraque, who had begun to scale Poorman's
Hill, imagined himself mounting once again his entire
existence.

He approached the summit. Already the slender spire of the Saint-Jean steeple, where he had been
married, could be made out, distinctly, pointed in the
sky. Then there was the octagonal tower of the cathe-
dral, farther away and hard to make out, whence the
wind carried a knell of lugubrious bells. Soon finally,
the entire town, amassing its houses in a pale ray of
setting winter sunlight, the mournful and mute town,
asleep in its green somber belt of old ramparts cov-

ered in ivy. Barely a little life, there below, beside the train station, where some red factory chimneys spewed some smoke. But here, outside the ramparts, at the very foot of Poorman's Hill, the cemetery: the crosses, a complete crowd of immobile and bizarre crosses, and, here and there, tufts of dark green cypress making the livid whiteness of the tombs stand out.

As if he had been summoned, he also, but by a letter of announcement that was not drawn up by M. Menu, and on which Eudoxe had not written the address, M. Fraque arrived on time. All Noirfond was there in front of him, nobility, bourgeoisie and the people, squeezing in at the gates of the cemetery following the hearse, as strongly curious as all Noirfond which, one evening, towards midnight, a half-century earlier, had crowded together at the town hall and at the church to see Zoé dressed in a white wedding gown. The town authorities were doubtless holding the cords of the pall. Isnard couldn't be walking far from the coffin. The doctor Boisvert, himself, was not a man to miss such a spectacle, no more than the rumormongers of the Circle, the cafe loafers, and the reading room members. Eudoxe, surrounded by rhetoricians and philosophers, probably made an impression with his monocle. Perhaps, brought together by chance in the crowd, separated by a simple tomb railing, the abbé de la Môle and the Protestant pastor regarded each other, like two mastiffs fighting over the same bone.

A swarm of people continued to arrive, even though the cemetery, now dark with people, seemed full, except for one spot where the hearse had stopped, next to a small mound of freshly dug earth. Despite his farsighted eyes, for several minutes, M. Fraque couldn't make out anything anymore. Standing at the top of Poorman's Hill, with one hand pressing on the cane, with the other hand acting in vain as a kind of aid to his vision, he didn't pick up his hat which had just fallen off his head, and a small breeze continued to drive his long white locks, at each instant, into his face. Suddenly, there, over there, at the rear of the hearse, a small cloud of dust was rising into the air and told him that it was all over. And he just stood there, feeling as though they had just thrown dirt, large shovelfuls of it, over fifty years of his life disappeared into the bottom of a hole.

Other Books by the Publisher

Fanchette's Pretty Little Foot by Restif de La Bretonne

Je M'Accuse... by Léon Bloy

My Hospitals & My Prisons by Paul Verlaine

Salvation Through the Jews by Léon Bloy

Words of a Demolitions Contractor by Léon Bloy

Cellulely by Paul Verlaine

Ecclesiastical Laurels by Jacques Rochette de la Morlière

Flowers of Bitumen by Émile Goudeau

Songs for Her & Odes in Her Honor by Paul Verlaine

On Huysmans' Tomb by Léon Bloy

Ten Years a Bohemian by Émile Goudeau

The Soul of Napoleon by Léon Bloy

Blood of the Poor by Léon Bloy

Joan of Arc and Germany by Léon Bloy

Theresa the Philosopher & The Carmelite Extern Nun by Marquis d'Argens & Anne-Gabriel Meusnier de Querlon

A Platonic Love by Paul Alexis
Two Novellas: Francine Cloarec's Funeral and Benjamin Rozes by Léon Hennique

The Revealer of the Globe: Christopher Columbus & His Future Beatification (Part One) by Léon Bloy

Héloïse Pajadou's Calvary by Lucien Descaves

An Immodest Proposal by Dr. Helmut Schleppend

The Pornographer by Restif de La Bretonne

Style (Theory and History) by Ernest Hello

On the Threshold of the Apocalypse: 1913-1915 by Léon Bloy

She Who Weeps (Our Lady of La Salette) by Léon Bloy

The Sylph by Claude Prosper Jolyot de Crébillon (*fils*)

School of Woman by Nicolas Chorier

Voyage in France by a Frenchman by Paul Verlaine

Ourigan, Oregon by William Clark, Richard Robinson, and anonymous

Drowning by Yu Dafu

Cull of April by Francis Vielé-Griffin

www.ingramcontent.com/pod-product-compliance
Lightning Source LLC
Chambersburg PA
CBHW030354180626
46812CB00007B/2873